GABRIELLA LEPORE

First published in Great Britain in 2015

This edition published in 2015 by
OF TOMES PUBLISHING
U N I T E D K I N G D O M

Book design by Inkstain Interior Book Designing
www.inkstainformatting.com

For James

...and all of our 2015 adventures!

BLACK HEATH

PROLOGUE

December

"**WHAT DO YOU** know about the Tomlins family?" Officer Bryant asked, folding his hands on the table as he scrutinised the girl in the seat opposite him.

The light bulb overhead flickered, casting strips of fluorescent light across the police station's cold, grey interrogation room.

On the other side of the table, Maggie Ellmes sat rigid in her chair. "Same as everyone else," she replied without missing a beat.

Bryant leaned back in his seat and smirked. "And what exactly is it that everyone else knows?"

Maggie swallowed. "Everyone in Blackheath knows the Tomlins family."

"Maximus Tomlins," Officer Bryant recounted as though he were reading from a personal ad. "Single dad, raising four boys all on his own. . ." The fractured bursts of light reflected in his eyes as he spoke.

Maggie nodded her head, dark blonde waves creeping like ivy over her school sweater.

"Blackheath High kids, right?" Bryant pressed.

Maggie nodded again.

"Tell me about them," Bryant prompted. Beads of perspiration had formed on his brow now; he needed more than this.

"Evan's the oldest," Maggie began. "He's eighteen and a senior. Then there's Joel, who's seventeen. Then Ainsley, who's thirteen, I think. And Pippin, of course. But he's only four or something."

"And Mrs Tomlins? What does *everyone* know about her?" Bryant was leaning forward now, pressing both palms flat against the table.

"No one knows what happened to Mrs Tomlins," Maggie answered. "Only that she cut and run. She left after Joel was born. I heard she came back for a while, but then left again not long after Ainsley was born."

"And?" Bryant pushed.

"And Mr Tomlins went to look for her."

"And then?"

Maggie shrugged. "And he never found her, I guess, so he just came home."

"What about Mrs Tomlins? Did she ever reappear?" Bryant's eyes bore into Maggie across the table. "She must have if there's a fourth child in the picture."

"She came back for a couple of months a few years ago, then disappeared again."

"And, lo and behold, a baby gets left on the Tomlins' doorstep nine months later," Bryant added.

"Pippin," said Maggie.

"How do you know all this?"

"I told you already. *Everyone* in Blackheath knows all this." Now it was Maggie's turn to lean forward. "And I know *you* know all this too, Officer. So I can't help but wonder why you're asking me."

Another lazy smirk. "Everyone knows the Tomlins are witches, too, don't they?" he suggested coolly. "That's why people are afraid of them, isn't it?"

Maggie held his gaze. "Are *you* afraid of them?"

He smiled darkly. "I think a more interesting question is, are *you*?"

ONE

The Witch House

AN OLD SILVER Jeep chugged along the winding roads of Blackheath. In the driver's seat sat a tired man with traces of coarse grey stubble and a face that looked worn, marked with wrinkles around eyes that had once been bright. In the front passenger seat sat a boy of eighteen, whose gentle features and neat blonde hair suggested that he was the peacemaker of the family. In the back of the Jeep sat the peacemaker's three younger brothers, varying in heights and appearance. In the middle was a boy of thirteen who bore the same fair colourings and soft features as his older brother. On his left side, strapped haphazardly into a car seat, was a stubby four-year-old with wide lavender eyes framed by long golden lashes.

And on his right side, gazing out the car window at the distant mountain peaks gleaming in the early-September sunshine, sat Joel.

Joel didn't quite share the same angelic appearance as his brothers; his hair, which was a shade or two darker than the others', had grown an inch or two too long and had nowhere to go but fall over his brow in unruly waves. His expression carried a certain heaviness—a jadedness that his brothers' faces did not. However, much like those of his three siblings, his eyes were a pale shade of violet.

"Max," Joel called to the man in the driver's seat. His tone was clipped and unfamiliar, as though he were talking to a stranger rather than his own father.

"Yes, Joel?" the tired man replied, meeting his son's gaze in the rear view mirror.

"You missed the turnoff," said Joel, rapping his knuckles on the Jeep's grimy back window to direct his father's gaze to a parched dirt road that led into the wooded hills.

Maximus's rough hands twitched on the steering wheel. He looked to his side, where his eldest son Evan was riding shotgun.

"Did we miss the turn, Evan?" he asked.

In the backseat, Joel rolled his eyes. "I just told you we did," he called up to his dad.

Still, Maximus looked to Evan for confirmation.

"I don't know," said Evan at last, his voice as smooth as velvet. "But if Joel said we did . . ." he trailed off.

Maximus gave a heavy sigh and pulled the Jeep over at the side of the road. Overhanging branches from nearby trees scraped against the Jeep's side windows as they came to a stop.

Ainsley, squashed awkwardly between Joel and Pippin, slipped his chunky headphones down around his neck. "Why are we stopping?" he demanded, peering over his four-year-old brother's head to get a look at the foliage that was pressing up against the windows. "Are we there?"

"No, we're not *there,*" Joel answered under his breath. "We missed the turnoff."

Pippin's doe eyes gleamed. "Turnoff," he repeated. "Joel?" he called to his brother.

"What is it, Pippin?" Joel asked wearily.

"Turnoff," said Pippin.

"Yes, Pippin. Turnoff," said Joel with a sigh.

Ainsley slipped his headphones back onto his ears, trapping wisps of ash blonde hair beneath the soft leather ear pads as he re-submerged himself in a bubble of thrash metal.

Joel ran a hand through his own hair, pushing some stray dark strands from his eyes. *I need a haircut*, he thought for what felt like the hundredth time that month. *Maybe I can cut it myself and skip the cost.* He frowned at the thought, contemplating the shoddy job he always seemed to do whenever he tried to cut Pippin's hair.

He glanced at his toddler brother's blonde curls, which were corkscrewing every which way but down.

Yeah, maybe not, Joel decided.

At least it was almost autumn now—carnival season in Blackheath. He'd be able to make some extra cash working the stalls on the weekends and in the evenings after school.

All of a sudden, Joel was brought back to the present when Maximus revved the Jeep. They made a U-turn on the deserted road, kicking up a cloud of dust as they set off back the way they'd come.

Not many other cars were on the road that day, which wasn't surprising, really. This part of town was always pretty quiet, with no houses or shops to speak of. And even though Blackheath was little more than a hamlet by anyone's account, now the Tomlins family was about to head even further away from civilisation. Deep into the hills on the outskirts of town for a new start. A new life.

A new home, Joel mused. *Wait, an old home*, he revised. *A crappy old home.*

He and Evan had visited the house once before, when Really Old Aunt Pearl had lived there. The two younger Tomlins brothers hadn't been born yet, though. Back then, it had just been Joel, Evan, Maximus, and. . .

Joel closed his eyes. He didn't need to think about his mother. Not today. Today was supposed to be the start of something new.

The Jeep slowly lumbered along the road for a while longer, narrowly dodging some low-hanging tree branches that bowed in their path.

"Here," Joel muttered, thumbing towards an even narrower path heading into the forest.

Maximus eased his foot off the accelerator and idled in the middle of the road, the engine purring in the quiet afternoon.

"Does this look right, Evan?" Maximus asked.

Again Joel rolled his eyes. "Yes, it's right," he said with a sharp breath. "I remember it."

Maximus glanced into the rear view mirror with a half-smile. "You were just a baby when we came here, Joel. How could you possibly remember it?"

"I was four," Joel corrected. "Kids remember things from that age." He caught sight of Pippin out of the corner of his eye. "Same age as Pip," he added. "The kid's probably going to remember everything about this day."

Pippin giggled to himself, causing his blonde curls to bounce into an even unrulier arrangement.

Maximus turned his attention back to Evan. "What do you think, son?"

Joel sighed.

Evan shrugged. "Sure."

"Turnoff," said Pippin.

And Maximus turned the wheel.

ARRIVING AT THE new house was a surreal moment for everyone. This place was home now, thanks to the passing of Really Old Aunt Pearl. It was time for the house to change hands, and on this particular occasion, it had skipped several generations and landed right in the lap of Evan Tomlins, heir to the property and the most promising young witch the family line had produced for centuries.

Yes, Maximus or any of his ample number of sisters, cousins, or extended family members might have been next in line for the house, technically speaking. But it was Evan who had secured it; for Evan Tomlins was the Chosen One—and none of the other Tomlins could ever forget that.

The Jeep rolled to a stop in the winding pathway that led up to the house—or, more accurately, the mansion. The five Tomlins inside the car looked out at the building, baulking in a mixture of awe and despair.

Really Old Aunt Pearl had left the place ramshackle, to say the least. It was a tall, black and grey expanse of a building, almost castle-like with its turrets and its balconies with rusted railings and its crumbling brickwork. Tree-sized shrubs had taken root all around it, blocking the various entrances, and crawling ivy had spun its ascending web up the walls to the various rooflines three and four stories above.

Joel's legs suddenly felt heavy as he stepped out of the Jeep and peered up at the crumbling window frames and their cracked leaded glass panes. Moving into a mansion, though fool-proof on paper, was more akin to *foolish* when standing before the decaying remains of Really Old Aunt Pearl's legacy.

Is it too soon to pine for our old compact split-level in downtown Blackheath? he wondered.

As Maximus busied himself unloading boxes from the trunk, Joel slung his rucksack over his shoulder and slowly approached the mansion. He could hear his breath escaping in nervous rasps.

Home, he thought. He swallowed against the dryness in his throat. *Bring it on.*

"You should give Dad a break," came a quiet voice from behind him.

Joel cast a sideways glance as Evan appeared next to him. "Why?" he shot back.

"He's trying his best."

Joel snorted. "With you, maybe. The Chosen One. Heir to Blackheath's most prestigious address."

They both turned to face the dilapidated front porch. Together they stared, transfixed, at the black iron door and brass lion's head doorknocker before them.

"Besides," Joel added under his breath, "it's Dad who gives *me* a hard time."

His gaze flickered to his brother for a moment. The boys stood at the same height, just passing six feet tall. But Evan stood taller somehow, lean and fair, with violet eyes so pale they almost appeared translucent in the misted sunshine.

"He doesn't mean to give you a hard time," Evan insisted, adjusting the weight of his rucksack on his shoulder. "And he's good to us, Joel. You know he is. He didn't have to come back, but he did."

I wish he hadn't *come back*, Joel thought. But he held his tongue.

"And when our mother comes back," Evan continued, "she'll have somewhere to call home—"

"We don't have a mother," Joel said at once. "Not anymore."

Evan winced.

Joel's heart gave a tug. "Sorry," he mumbled.

Calmly, Evan returned his attention to the house. "Shall we go inside?"

Joel wrinkled his nose as he took in the old mansion's derelict veranda railing. "Are you sure you want to?"

Evan grinned and began towards the porch. He climbed gingerly up the first of three broken front steps. "She'll come back one day," he commented over his shoulder. "Just like Dad did."

Joel cast a glance back to the Jeep, where Ainsley and Pippin were hovering at Maximus's side as he unpacked the car.

I hope not, he thought, then began silently after Evan.

Using both hands, Evan yanked on the iron door handle. The door lurched open with a shriek. The two boys stepped inside a dark, dank entrance hall. They stared, dumbfounded, at the wide sweeping staircase, its broken banister lit up with streaks of speckled sunlight leaking through the un-shuttered windows.

Swapping a grimace, the brothers ventured farther inside, their shoes crunching on debris and tumbled down glass shards as they made for the staircase.

"This place is . . ." Joel began, running his fingers along the dusty banister.

"It has . . ." Evan added.

"Something," Joel managed.

"Definitely something," Evan finished.

Side by side, they treaded warily up the wide staircase, carefully avoiding the missing third step. When they reached the top, they did a matched double-take as a rat scurried across their path.

"Rats," Joel noted, his voice echoing hauntingly off the high ceilings.

"Rat," Evan corrected. "Singular."

Joel raised an eyebrow and they forged on.

They walked from room to room, systematically opening doors and peering inside each chamber, trying not to breathe in the moth ball scent. At the end of the long hallway, they came to a room with two narrow single beds lined up against the rear wall and a tiny balcony off a set of ancient French doors. Without thinking, they tossed their rucksacks onto the beds, Evan claiming the one on the left and Joel claiming the one on the right. With that done, they turned and stood face to face.

"So, congratulations," said Joel with false enthusiasm. "You've arrived at your palace, Chosen One. Do these quarters meet your princely standards, or should I lay out my jacket for you to walk on?" He laughed at his own joke.

For once, Evan wasn't smiling. His handsome face drew into a scowl. "Would you quit it with that *Chosen One* crap already? I'm getting really sick of it, Joel."

"What?" Joel made a show of looking confused. "But . . . you *are* the Chosen One, aren't you?"

Evan exhaled sharply. "And you're not, right? Is that it? You're jealous, so you want me to feel as bad as you do?"

Joel laughed again—though this time, the sound was far from genial. "Jealous?" he fumed. "You actually think I'm *jealous* of you, Chosen One?"

Evan bristled. "You can't stand that I—"

"I can't stand that your ego is so inflated that—"

"You can't stand that I'm better than you at—"

"I can't stand that you *think* you're better than me at—"

"Everything," the boys finished in unison.

"Because I am," Evan said, holding Joel's gaze. "I am better than you at everything. Is that what you want? For me to say it?"

Joel's expression hardened.

"Because I *am* the Chosen One," Evan finished. "So get used to it."

Joel threw up his hands. "So you can do a couple of fancy spells," he mocked. "So what? Can you fix *this?*" He nodded to the cracked plastering at the top of the nearest wall and the water damage surrounding it. "No, huh? So what exactly *can* you do, Evan? Make it rain? Big deal."

Over their heads, an aged chandelier began to tremble, showering decades of dust over the floorboards.

"Okay," Evan bit back, his hands balling into fists. "Then you're just jealous because Dad and I—"

"Don't!" Joel shouted at the same instant that one of the chandelier's light bulbs shattered. "Don't even finish that sentence. Or so help me god, Evan, I'll—"

At that moment, someone cleared their throat. The boys turned to see Maximus standing in the bedroom doorway, holding Pippin's hand while Ainsley stood behind him.

The chandelier stopped trembling.

Maximus was wearing a strained smile. "Boys," he said, holding up a palm. "Fighting already, Joel?"

Joel grimaced.

"Let's try to get along for now, shall we?" Maximus suggested with forced brightness. "This is supposed to be the fun part."

Oh, so this *is the fun part?* Joel thought disparagingly.

"Don't you want to choose your rooms?" Maximus asked.

"Already have," muttered Joel.

"This one's fine," Evan added, touching the musty bedspread.

"Yeah," Joel echoed, his gaze cast downwards. "This will do."

Maximus let out a genuine laugh. "You boys don't have to share a room anymore if you don't want to. This is a mansion. Hell, you can have two rooms each if you want!"

Ainsley gave a whoop of delight.

Caught up in the excitement, Pippin yelled, "Turnoff!"

Joel and Evan fell quiet. All of a sudden, the anger between them melted away. They blinked at each other across the silence.

"Oh," said Evan after a moment. "Right. Yeah. I guess we're just so used to sharing . . ."

"Well, yeah," Joel agreed. "We've always shared a room. But now we don't have to." He mustered a smile.

"Good," said Evan, mirroring his brother's expression. "Great."

"Yeah. Great."

They fell into another silence. Neither one moved.

Maximus laughed again. "Well?" he prompted. "What's the holdup? Go choose your new rooms."

"Okay." Evan picked up his rucksack from the leftmost bed. "You can have this room, if you want," he told Joel. "I'll . . . um . . . choose a different one."

"Yeah, sure," Joel said hoarsely. "Thanks, Evan. I'll . . ." he hesitated. "I'll be sure to enjoy it."

With that settled, Maximus, Ainsley, and Pippin disappeared down the dingy upstairs corridor. Before following, Evan paused beneath the strip of sunlight lancing in through the grubby French doors. He offered his hand for Joel to shake.

"See you around," he said.

"Yeah," Joel replied, shaking his brother's hand. "See you around."

TWO

Joyless's Victims

MAGGIE RACED THROUGH the orchard, hugging her school books to her chest. She ran along the pathway as it snaked through the apple trees, dodging the last of the season's fallen apples as she headed for the old grey stone building beyond the boundary walls.

Ahead, a domed annex marked the entrance to the school, an outer corridor which formed a tunnel into the imposing gothic-era building. The stately school never ceased to impress Maggie—despite the fact she'd seen it every day of her life for the past seven years. Even on weekends she had a clear view of the building from the window of her dorm room in the boarding house on the other side of the orchard.

By the time she reached the annex, Maggie was breathless and chilled from the cool October air. She scuttled through the passageway, her footsteps echoing off the domed mosaic ceiling.

Flinging open the stained glass doors at the far end, she hurried into the school's main corridor.

It was quiet. Way too quiet. The first bell had already gone and everyone was in class. Meaning that Maggie would have to do the walk of shame into homeroom and have Mr Fitzpatrick yell at her in front of everyone. Again.

Thanks a bunch for waking me, Isla, she thought with a grimace.

Didn't Isla know that the point of having a roommate was to eradicate the need for an alarm clock?

FitzP is going to kill me, Maggie thought, shuddering as she pictured Mr Fitzpatrick's face turning purple and veiny like it always did when he was mad.

"Maggie Ellmes," rasped a voice from across the corridor. It was swiftly followed by the familiar clip-clop of high heeled shoes.

Maggie's stomach lurched. *Joyless*, she thought.

"Morning, Ms Joy," she said aloud. She turned to face her opponent and attempted to dazzle her with a bright smile.

Ms Joy glowered back, her beady eyes magnified behind rectangular spectacles and her black hair scraped into a tight bun.

Maggie touched her own messy bun, trying to subtly fix a few of the wayward dark blonde strands with her index finger. Joyless was big on presentation.

"You're late," Ms Joy snapped. "Sign in." She thrust a clipboard on top of the grade eleven books piled in Maggie's arms.

Maggie groaned inwardly. Signing in meant that her attendance record for that morning would read as an absence. Which meant consequences. Which meant, in layman's terms, after-school detention.

She exhaled in despair. "But . . . I'm not *that* late, am I?"

She glanced up at the huge clock that was suspended from the ceiling above the main entrance. *Yeesh. I guess I* am *that late.*

Joyless tapped her long red fingernail on the clipboard and let out a squawk of disapproval.

"But . . ." Maggie began feebly.

Joyless's narrow eyes widened behind her thick lenses and her expression hardened to steel.

Sighing sadly, Maggie shifted the weight of her books to one arm. She wearily took the pen from the clipboard and tagged her name onto the end of a sizeable list of Joyless's victims, then awkwardly nudged the clipboard back towards her.

Joyless raised her pointy chin and double checked the signature, looking down her nose at the sign-in sheet.

"Let this be a lesson to you," she chided. "Maybe next time you'll arrive to school on time."

Maggie sighed again.

Right, she thought grudgingly. *Like* that's *ever going to happen.*

MAGGIE SLIPPED INTO homeroom and closed the door behind her with a quiet click. The students were already in their seats, but talking casually amongst themselves while they waited for their absent teacher.

No FitzP, Maggie realised. If only Joyless hadn't busted her, she would have been home free. She dropped irritably into the first empty desk closest to the door—a desk usually reserved for the one person whose chronic lateness exceeded even Maggie's: Joel Tomlins.

Today, though, Joel was nowhere in sight and the desk was Maggie's. She craned her neck to look back into the classroom to where her friends were huddled in the back row, whispering between one another with Isla in the centre.

Maggie thumped her desk, trying to catch her roommate's attention. Isla glanced over and waved a greeting. Her long black hair fell in a sleek braid over her thin shoulder as she sat at her desk with impeccably straight posture.

"Why didn't you wake me?" Maggie mouthed over the heads of the rows of students between them.

"Student Council meeting," Isla mouthed back. "Early. New Boy." Her coffee-brown eyes twinkled.

Maggie quickly scanned the room. She noted the usual gathering of her homeroom classmates. No new boy, though.

She frowned and held up her palms to Isla.

"The grade below," Isla clarified soundlessly. "Miss Price's class."

A few of the other girls in the back row erupted into fits of giggles just as Mr Fitzpatrick burst breathlessly into the classroom. He swung his briefcase onto the oak teacher's desk at the front of the class and wiped beads of sweat from his brow.

His shirt and tie looked a little askew and his thinning copper hair was stuck flat to his forehead.

"Good morning," he greeted the class distractedly.

The voices simmered and focus shifted to Mr Fitzpatrick as he shuffled through a mound of papers on his desk in search of the elusive register. After he'd unearthed it from a pile of paperwork and elastic bands, he began reading the names aloud to an echo of unenthusiastic responses.

"Maggie Ellmes," he called without looking up.

"Here," she grumbled.

Damn Joyless, she thought bitterly, bristling at the injustice. *This is totally unfair. Even Mr Fitzpatrick is later than me.*

Mr Fitzpatrick continued with the roll call. When he reached Joel Tomlins, the classroom door swung open and, right on cue, Joel appeared. At seventeen, he was tall and broad. His medium brown hair was rumpled, as if he'd just rolled out of bed. His shirt was unbuttoned at the top, and his tie was fastened around the collar with just a loose knot. The last few inches of a candy bar—presumably his breakfast—were clenched between his teeth, while one hand supported the nearly empty backpack that was slung over his shoulder. His other hand casually rested on the doorframe as he surveyed the room.

His stare landed on Maggie, and he frowned. He took one more bite of the candy bar before tossing the rest of it into the wastepaper basket.

"You're in my seat," he said to her, raising an eyebrow.

"So?" Maggie laced her fingers together on the desktop. "You don't own it. Go sit somewhere else."

Mr Fitzpatrick paused his roll call to cast a formidable glare at Joel. "There's an empty seat over there, Mr Tomlins," he said, gesturing to a desk on the other side of the room.

After a bated moment, Joel let out a heavy sigh and manoeuvred his way through the room towards the desk by the window. He muttered something under his breath as he dropped his backpack to the floor and sank into the empty seat.

Maggie flinched and sat up a little straighter. What had Joel just said?

He'd better not be putting a spell on me, she thought crossly, sneaking a glance at him.

The autumn sunlight was streaking through the trees beyond the window, casting rainbows across Joel's hair.

Is he hexing me right now? she wondered. *He'd better not be hexing me.*

The Tomlins boys *were* witches, after all. Their father, too. Okay, so there wasn't any proof, but it was common knowledge. They didn't try to hide it or deny it, either. Not that they could ever cover up the fact that all the Tomlins boys made the wind stir and the tree branches tremble whenever they were near. Or the conspicuous detail that they all had strange lavender coloured eyes which seemed to darken to black intermittently.

But, Maggie reasoned with herself, they'd been in class together for the past seven years, and he hadn't put a spell on her yet—not to her knowledge, anyway.

She shivered and stole one last peek at him.

A light breeze from the open window tousled his already rumpled hair, toying with the strands. His violet gaze was on Mr Fitzpatrick now as the teacher resumed calling the register.

"Charlie Wells?"

"Yo, FitzP," Charlie returned from the back of the room. A basketball was sitting on top of his desk and he was resting his chin on it as though contemplating a nap. Beefed-up with muscles and sporting a buzz cut, Charlie lazily fist-pumped the air.

"And Isla Williams?" Mr Fitzpatrick concluded.

"Present," Isla sang out sweetly.

Mr Fitzpatrick closed the register book just as the bell rang to signal the end of homeroom. Chairs scraped and chatter resumed. While her classmates swarmed around her, pushing towards the doorway to get out, Maggie remained at her desk, waiting for Isla and the others.

As Joel passed by, he placed his hand on the desk possessively. A warning, she knew.

Maggie flicked his fingers away.

He withdrew his hand and scowled. "Who said you could touch me?"

"Oh, get over yourself, Joel," she groused. "It's just a seat. And P.S., I wouldn't touch you if you were the last guy on earth." She folded her arms across her chest and feigned a retching motion.

Joel rolled his eyes, then turned and made his way out of the classroom with Charlie and a few other guys in tow.

Finally Maggie rose to her feet as Isla approached, flanked by Blonde Lauren and Hilary.

"I think Joel Tomlins put a spell on me," Maggie grumbled, running her fingertips across her face to check for warts and boils.

Blonde Lauren's powder blue eyes widened. "For real?"

Even Hilary's perfected hipster mask of perpetual boredom wavered slightly.

Maggie nodded sadly.

"Of course he didn't put a spell on you," Isla chided with a musical giggle. She flipped her dark silken braid to reveal a baby pink button over her heart that read *Vote Isla Williams for Homecoming Queen!* in bedazzled letters. There was no question that everyone would vote for her, though. She won it every year.

The girls left the classroom in a convoy, venturing into the bustling corridor.

"Science," Isla said with a groan as she linked her arm through Maggie's. "Then Maths."

Maggie's shoulders slumped. "Mondays suck. And Joyless made me sign her Victims List."

Blonde Lauren and Hilary gave a chorus of commiserative noises.

"Aw," Isla sympathised with a pretty pout. "She caught you, huh?"

"Yes, and it's totally unjust!" Maggie declared. "If FitzP didn't care, then why should she? Because she's a sadist, that's why."

The trio of girls nodded their heads in solidarity as they strolled towards the Science block.

Hilary rolled her eyes behind her oversized geek-chic glasses. "Joyless thrives off forcing her bourgeois conformist conceptions down the throats of freethinkers. Her sole purpose in life is to brainwash the heretic masses."

"Exactly!" Maggie agreed—at least, she assumed she agreed. Some of Hilary's lingo was lost on her. "Joyless hates my free thoughts so she's trying to brainwash me! Maybe Student Council could do something about it?" she suggested, looking hopefully to Isla. "You know, clear my name?" She brightened a little at the thought.

Isla smiled vaguely, clearly having no intention of acting on the request. Instead, she wiggled her finely shaped eyebrows and said, "I know what will cheer you up."

Maggie's shoulders sagged. "What?" she grumbled.

"Well," Isla began, glancing between the girls, "don't quote me on this, but I'm pretty certain we've got third period with New Guy! He's super smart and apparently he's skipped a grade for some of his classes."

Maggie folded her arms. "Wow," she remarked dryly.

"Wait til you see him," Blonde Lauren gushed.

Maggie remained deadpan. "Does anyone know New Guy's name?"

"Kaden," Blonde Lauren answered dreamily.

"Kaden Fallows," Isla purred, not to be outdone.

"Is he really that big of a deal?" Maggie asked as they followed the flow of people towards the Chemistry lab.

"Yes," all three girls replied in unison.

Maggie's eyes widened when she noticed that even Hilary had cracked a coy smile. Hilary—the same girl who normally took pride in ridiculing any form of boy talk, deeming it a step backwards for feminism.

"Hil," Maggie gasped. "You, too?"

Hilary mustered a non-committal shrug. "He's okay, I guess. If you're into that metro urbanite kind of thing."

"He's perfect," Isla declared, her warm brown eyes gleaming. "You have to see him, Maggie. You'll die."

THE BELL RANG loudly at three o'clock. While the other students swarmed the mosaic-tiled corridor heading out into what was left of the alluring October sunlight, Maggie was hauling herself in the opposite direction. The direction of doom and misery.

With a heavy sigh, she opened the door to Ms Joy's classroom—or, more accurately, her Dungeon of Joylessness—and stepped inside.

Ms Joy was at her post at the teacher's desk in the front of the room, where she could keep a beady eye on the rows of single desks lined up before her. A number of Joyless's victims were already occupying several of the desks, one of whom was—

Joel Tomlins, Maggie realised. *Ugh.*

He barely glanced up at her as she slumped into her seat on the opposite side of the room.

As it happened, she hadn't always disliked Joel. And she didn't totally dislike him now, truth be told. But they travelled in different circles, and Joel's circle was... *meh*, Maggie decided. Jocks and cheerleaders.

I could be a cheerleader, if I wanted to, she thought, tapping her pencil on her chin as she stared into space. *I mean, how hard could it be?*

She extended a leg beneath the desk, envisioning a high kick.

Joyless cleared her throat and glowered.

Right, Maggie noted. *No moving of any kind.*

With a resigned sigh, she turned her attention to her notebook and pretended to concentrate on an imaginary assignment.

Doodling, she thought back to when she had first arrived at Blackheath. She'd been ten years old. Up until then, she'd lived with her grandparents in the city. But they were old—*seriously old,* Maggie reflected—and they weren't able to care for her anymore. Her mother had been living in France and her father had been acutely AWOL, so her grandparents had set up a trust fund to put her through school. That's how she'd ended up in Blackheath High's boarding house. And it wasn't so bad, either. She and Isla had been roommates for three years straight now, and it was like having a sister. A *family.*

Although every holiday, when Isla went home to visit her real family, Maggie found herself alone again.

She glanced across the room at Joel. He was spinning a pen between his fingers, staring out the window at the autumn leaves tumbling in the breeze.

There had been a time when she and Joel had actually been friends—well, sort of. Forced together by circumstance as the only kids their age left in Blackheath over the summer, they'd formed a kind of alliance. Having Joel around throughout those months had made being alone a little more bearable. But then they'd grown up, and grown apart. Needless to say, things were different now. Summers were different now.

Suddenly, as if hearing her thoughts, Joel glanced over at her. Maggie quickly looked away.

Better not make eye contact, she decided prudently, still wary from their encounter earlier that day. *I wouldn't want him to put a spell on me. Or would I?*

She paused, gazing thoughtfully between Ms Joy and Joel. A mischievous smile formed on her coral-pink lips.

Hastily scanning the classroom to ensure that she wasn't being watched by any of Joyless's Victims, who were presently either working on assignments or else just pretending to work on assignments, Maggie formulated an escape plan. Okay, so it would be risky, and Tomlins definitely wouldn't like it. However, she decided it was worth the risk regardless.

Sorry, Joel, but a Victim's got to do what a Victim's got to do . . .

With that, Maggie threw her pen across the room. It hit the blackboard behind Ms Joy's desk and fell to the floor with a clatter.

Ms Joy jumped, startled. Her hawkish eyes shot up from her paperwork.

"Hey!" Maggie exclaimed, staring pointedly at Joel.

Joel, who like everyone else in the room had glanced up to see what the ruckus was all about, frowned in confusion.

"Why did you do that?" Maggie accused him, batting her eyelashes innocently.

Joel's frown lines deepened. "Do what?"

Joyless rose from her chair. "Ms Ellmes," she scolded gruffly. "Just what do you think you're—"

"Ouch," Maggie groaned, gripping her forearm and drawing it to her chest. "Joel, stop it! Okay, I'm sorry! I'm sorry, alright? Just stop, please!"

The other Victims began to murmur amongst themselves. It took all of Maggie's willpower to keep from smiling when she heard the words 'spell' and 'witch' being whispered around the room.

She stole a glance at Ms Joy, who by now was looking utterly dumbfounded, her gaze darting between Maggie and Joel.

"Ms Joy, help me!" Maggie added for effect. "Tell him to stop!"

Joel's violet eyes darkened. "Shut up, Maggie."

Ms Joy regained what was salvageable of her composure. "Joel," she managed with an ever-so-slight quaver. "Please stop w-whatever it is that you're d-doing."

He groaned. "I'm not *doing* anything."

"Oh, Ms Joy!" Maggie wailed, gripping her arm tighter and rocking back and forth in her seat. "He's trying to make me pay for"—she paused to slip in a perfectly timed little whimper—"stealing his seat in homeroom."

The peanut gallery began to utter sentiments like 'oh my god' and 'it's true,' causing Maggie to glow with satisfaction. She could almost taste the freedom.

"She's lying!" Joel spluttered, throwing up his hands—and, Maggie noticed, a choice finger.

"Oww," Maggie sobbed. "Ms Joy . . . I need . . . to leave . . ."

"Yes," agreed Ms Joy, flustered. "Yes, Maggie, go. Go." She adjusted her spectacles and waved at Maggie to leave.

Maggie rose with much effort from her seat and, still hunched over in supposed pain, bundled her notebook and shoulder bag into her arms before hobbling to the door.

It was an Oscar-worthy performance if ever there was one at Blackheath High.

"Joel," Maggie heard Ms Joy saying, "any more of this behaviour and you'll be in the isolation block for the rest of the month!"

Ooh, brutal, thought Maggie, with only the smallest pang of remorse.

She stole a glance over her shoulder back into the Dungeon of Joylessness. Everyone's attention was on Joel now—but the only person Joel was looking at was Maggie.

A tiny smiled tugged at the corner of Maggie's lips. "Thanks, Joel," she mouthed. "I owe you one."

Joel's jaw dropped as Maggie darted out the doorway and down the corridor to freedom.

THREE

Red Energy

JOEL SWUNG THE family Jeep along the dirt path and came to a stop in the clearing in front of the old mansion. He cut the engine and sighed at the dismal building before him. Even after a whole month, he still hadn't been able to get used to coming home to this ramshackle heap of bricks.

"Come on, Ainsley," he muttered to his younger brother, who was sitting in the passenger seat.

This was the first year that Ainsley had been allowed to ride shotgun. Normally, Joel and Evan took the front seats on the school run. But since Evan had been so busy being the Chosen One lately, school runs weren't high on his agenda. Joel didn't mind, though. As far as he was concerned, Ainsley was marginally more tolerable than Evan at the moment. For a start, he was only thirteen, so he never got to drive the Jeep—which meant that Joel never had to engage in rock, paper, scissors before taking the wheel. Besides, ever since Evan had turned eighteen and been appointed Chosen, he'd been. . .

"Ugh," Ainsley groaned, interrupting Joel's reverie. "This place is a dump." Beneath perfectly corkscrewed blonde curls, his face puckered in disgust. "I mean, seriously," he added before swearing under his breath.

"Watch your language," Joel muttered.

To the outside world, Ainsley may have looked like a perfect little angel. *But, be warned,* Joel mused. *This one bites.*

"Anyway, this hell-pit is your home now," Joel reminded him. "So get used to it." With that, he pulled the keys from the ignition and swung open the driver's side door.

"It won't be my home for much longer," Ainsley remarked as he trailed after Joel along the wooded path towards the mansion's main door.

"Oh, yeah?" Joel replied as the wind whipped his umber coloured hair across his brow. "How do you figure? You plotting an escape, young one?"

"Maybe," Ainsley returned brightly as they climbed the poorly patched front steps. "I'm pretty sure I'm destined for bigger and better things."

"Well, good luck to you," Joel muttered as he slung his backpack over his shoulder and followed Ainsley inside.

They made their way towards the kitchen, sidestepping the broken floorboards as they went.

The kitchen was a long rectangular room overlooking the forest. It seemed lighter than most of the other rooms, with big windows, a huge stove, and rows of mismatched cupboards. Through the centre ran a table, where Alleged Aunt Topaz was sitting, polishing her crystal ball.

Not unlike all the other aunts, she was only an 'alleged' aunt because no one really knew which branch of the family tree she'd come from. Various 'aunts' had appeared over time, claiming family status only so they could subsequently claim coven status—and the Tomlins family was the best coven within a one hundred mile radius. Which wasn't saying much, since they were also the *only* coven within a one hundred mile radius. Therefore, every ageing witch within the perimeters of Blackheath was conveniently an 'aunt' or an 'uncle,' sometimes twice removed, and almost always related to their Alleged Great Uncle John. Though the real Tomlins clan had never even met this supposed great uncle, he was purportedly out there somewhere, spawning progeny like no tomorrow.

"Ainsley, my favourite child," Alleged Aunt Topaz rasped, casting her crooked nose and narrow gaze towards the younger boy. "Come here and let me use your most favourable energy."

Basking in the praise, Ainsley sank into a seat at the table, ready to be adored. He waved his hands above the crystal ball and began to hum.

Joel let his backpack slip to the floor with a thump. "What about me?" he exclaimed, extending his arms. "Am I invisible today or something? What's wrong with *my* energy?"

"Your energy is red," Alleged Aunt Topaz grunted. "It repels. I need the good stuff."

Maggie, Joel fumed silently.

"She spoiled my energy," he added out loud. "It was fine this morning."

Ainsley and Alleged Aunt Topaz tore their attention away from the crystal ball and turned to Joel, waiting for him to elaborate.

Joel exhaled tautly. "Man, she gets under my skin. I have these . . . feelings for her," he rambled, pacing around the kitchen table, circling Ainsley and Alleged Aunt Topaz like a shark. "These *hateful* feelings."

"For whom, dear?" Alleged Aunt Topaz asked.

"For Maggie," Joel spat. "Maggie Ellmes."

Ainsley made some noises of agreement. "Same here," he said. "I hate Maggie Ellmes, too. She's so . . . *pretty*. I want to dip her in dirt or something."

Joel pursed his lips. That wasn't it. But he couldn't put his finger on what *it* was, exactly. After all, when Maggie had first moved to Blackheath, they'd been friends—or a tenuous version of friends, at least. They would ignore each other nine months of the year, but when summer rolled around—when all the other kids at the boarding house had gone home, back to their families—Maggie and Joel would become allies once again. They'd build dens in the forest and invent complex games with ever-bending rules. But then they'd gotten older, and life had gotten more complex.

Then one summer, a few years ago, Maggie hadn't come to call for him, and he hadn't gone looking for her, either. They were officially teenagers, and their tenure as childhood playmates had expired.

Joel paused his circling for a second, then resumed. Alleged Aunt Topaz's tiny eyes followed him. They were somehow always on him, even when he was behind her.

"She's not *pretty*, Ainsley," Joel said through gritted teeth. "She's evil. Pure evil."

Alleged Aunt Topaz scowled at him. "Enough!" she sniped, stopping him in his tracks. "You're infecting the sacred area with your rancid red energy. Be gone, Joel Tomlins! And take your redness with you!"

He began to feel the pressure of Alleged Aunt Topaz's will weighing on him, as though an invisible force was pushing him away from the table.

"Where's Evan?" Joel asked, taking a step backwards.

"With Maximus."

Typical, thought Joel.

"And where's Maximus?" he asked, edging even closer to the hallway.

"With Evan. Now be gone, Joel Tomlins," Alleged Aunt Topaz ordered again. "Be gone until you aren't so unpleasant."

With a final surge, Joel felt himself being driven from the kitchen. He submitted to it and left without complaint. He'd already faced enough resistance for one day.

JOEL LUMBERED UP the staircase, avoiding the cracks in the treads and brushing aside cobwebs from the banister.

He made a beeline for his room and collapsed onto the bed. Staring up at the ceiling, he glared at the light fixture. What had once been an elegant chandelier was now layered with dust and grime. To his eyes, it looked like a set of twisted brown arms reaching out towards him threateningly.

Joel raised his palms up towards it and it began to sway gently, showering dust over the bed. Coughing, he waved away the particles with his hand and the chandelier stopped moving.

Heaving a sigh, Joel reached into his jacket pocket. He retrieved a crumpled piece of paper and unfolded it.

Soccer Tryouts, the heading read.

He withdrew a pen from his jeans pocket and pulled off the cap with his teeth. Smoothing the paper against his thigh, he underlined the time and place: Friday at 4:00 p.m. He needed an after-school activity to boost his school credits, and anything that kept him away from this house was a bonus. Actually, anything that kept him away from *Maximus* was a bonus.

Ever since Maximus had returned, everything had changed. He and Evan had been fine on their own, taking care of the younger ones by themselves. Why did Maximus bother coming back at all? *Just to take Evan away*, Joel decided grudgingly.

Anyway, the autumn carnival was starting that Friday, so at least he could get out of the house by working the rides every weekend for the next few months.

To anyone else, spending the weekends working might have sounded like the short straw. But to Joel, the carnival was home. In fact, the entire Tomlins family played a big part in the carnival. Not just Joel's immediate family, but his vast extended family as well. Alleged Aunt Topaz and her alleged sisters each had a booth at the carnival, along with all their various alleged offspring—none of whom Joel particularly liked, but who were family all the same. Allegedly.

They were the Blackheath Witches, as far as anyone else was concerned.

Joel smiled and the chandelier began to sway again.

FOUR

Skills

JOEL DRIED HIS hair with a towel in the locker room on Friday after soccer tryouts. He propped his foot up on the bench and laced up his sneakers, quietly confident as he listened to the other hopefuls second-guess their performances.

He felt a sturdy slap on his shoulder. "You nailed it, Buddy!"

Joel looked up to see Charlie Wells giving him a knowing smirk. Joel stood up and grinned back at him.

"You did alright, too," he replied.

"I'm calling this team," Charlie said under his breath, while numerous other candidates filtered in and out of the shower block. "Me, you, Henderson, Lomax, Wyatt..." He continued reeling off a list of his predicted teammates while Joel chewed over the possibilities.

Yeah, Joel mused. *This is sounding like a good, solid team...*

Suddenly his attention strayed to the locker room door, which swung open to reveal Evan venturing cautiously inside. The door fell shut behind him with a resounding thud.

Across the room, a cheer broke out from Coach Andrews. "Tomlins! Better late than never!"

Joel frowned. *I'm Tomlins, too . . .* he thought. *Or perhaps Tomlins Two,* he corrected with a grimace.

Charlie abandoned his conversation with Joel and turned towards the doorway, flashing a wide, toothy grin. "Tomlins!" he yelled. "You're trying out? My man! We got this season in the bag now!"

Evan just stood there with a refined smile on his blemish-free face, a slight blush rising in his cheeks. "No, I'm not trying out this year," he answered.

The statement was met by a chorus of outraged boos.

Joel pursed his lips.

Coach's bushy eyebrows knotted together beneath his bald, glistening head. "Son," he said to Evan, touching his snug-fitting XL polo shirt above the heart. "Think about it, please. We've got a shot at the championship this year, although"—he attempted to lower his voice, but years of hollering at players had totally skewed his sense of volume—"without you, we've got no hope."

It took every ounce of self-restraint Joel had not to scowl.

"Sorry, Coach," said Evan, squirming in discomfort under the coach's beseeching gaze. "Really, I am, but I just can't. I've got too much school work this year."

School work? thought Joel. *Yeah, right.* Evan had barely been in class since the semester started. He was too preoccupied with being the Chosen One.

"Then why'd you come down here?" Coach asked with strained good humour. "To torture us or something?"

Evan smiled. "I was just watching my little brother try out."

Around the locker room, a few mildly interested gazes flickered to Joel before returning to Evan.

Huh? Joel thought, surprised. He'd never looked into the bleachers. He hadn't thought there'd be any point.

"You did great, Joel," said Evan as he began to weave through the people on his way towards his brother.

Joel busied himself re-tying his sneakers. "Thanks," he muttered without looking up.

A silence fell between them.

When the silence was just about to draw on for a second too long, Joel stood up to face his brother eye to eye. "So," he said, clearing his throat, "are you working the carnival tonight?"

"Yeah," said Evan. "I'm on a stall. You?"

"Yeah," said Joel. "I'm on the Haunted House."

They both broke into matching grins, and for a split second the boys were like mirror images of each other. The mention of the Haunted House always seemed to have that effect on them, bringing out a playfulness between them that often got forgotten these days. Especially since they'd moved into Really Old Aunt Pearl's house.

"Dad let me borrow the Jeep," said Evan. "You want a ride?"

"Sure," answered Joel as he moved towards his locker. "Let me just get my bag."

"Cool. I'm picking up Dad on the way."

Joel froze. His fingers fiddled with the combination on his locker while he considered Evan's words. "Actually," he said at last, "I think I'll walk."

Evan's handsome face pulled down into a frown. "Joel . . ."

"I should walk," Joel explained, retrieving his rucksack from the locker. "I need the warm-down anyway." He slammed the metal door shut, and the clang reverberated against the locker room's cement walls. "I'll see you there, okay?"

"Okay," Evan muttered. "But . . ."

Joel started heading for the exit without waiting for his brother to finish. "Oh, and Evan?" he called over his shoulder.

"Yeah?" Evan replied, his tone rising quizzically.

"Thanks for coming."

JOEL LEFT THE school and began walking along the narrow path leading through the orchard. Stone walls circled the campus and, up ahead, an archway carved into the stonework marked the exit of the school grounds. Autumn leaves had begun to fall, scattering across the pathway like crisp flames.

A chill moved through Joel as he crossed beneath the stone archway and emerged out onto the quiet streets of Blackheath. He could walk to the carnival from here. In truth, he would enjoy the walk. It was only a couple of miles, and besides, he liked the sensation of the cool breeze wrapping around him.

Joel closed his eyes for a moment, trusting his instincts to guide his way. Content in his solitude, he listened to the rustle of birds moving through the thickets and the sound of church bells chiming in the distance.

After a few moments he came to a standstill and slowly opened his eyes. He was alone. The school was concealed behind the looming stone wall behind him, and the street was otherwise deserted. With a deep breath, he focused on a nearby tree that had yet to shed its leaves.

Its branches stirred in response to his gaze.

Joel shivered as he felt the familiar rush of witchcraft move through his veins. Drawing in a quick breath, his body gave a tremor. He could feel a flood of electricity rocking through him, building inside of him with a flutter of urgency, bliss . . . and power.

"Fall," Joel whispered.

On his command, a gust of wind funnelled through the street and wrapped itself around the tree. It rattled the branches and loosened the leaves from their nodes, freeing them and sending them showering down over Joel and the pavement.

A rasp of breath escaped Joel's lips and he laughed.

"Joel?" came a voice from behind, startling him.

He spun around.

"Maggie," he said tightly, swallowing as her pale green eyes bore into him. He was still peeved about what she'd pulled on him in detention a few days before.

"That was weird," she said, turning her gaze upon the now bare branches of the tree.

Joel held his composure. "It was, wasn't it?"

She took a step closer to him, her movements cautious. "What are you doing hanging around here so late, anyway?" she probed suspiciously. "School finished hours ago. Haven't you got a home to go to?"

"Yeah, I do," Joel shot back, shifting the weight of his backpack on his shoulder. "Which is more than I can say for you."

He winced when he noticed the aura around her shift and fade. Where just moments ago her energy had been easy and light, it now darkened around her in a pained way.

Sorry, he wanted to say. But no words came out.

She gathered herself and folded her arms over her chest. "I wouldn't brag about your *home* if I were you," she said defensively. "From what I've heard, your new house is a creepy old hell-pit for witches."

Joel smiled in spite of the affront—mostly because that was exactly how he described the place, too.

"What are you doing out here, anyway?" he returned the question. "Are you following me?"

"Pah!" she spluttered. "In your dreams, maybe. And not that it's any of your business, but I'm going to the carnival."

Joel raised an eyebrow. "Oh, so you *are* following me, then."

Maggie's eyes narrowed. "No," she replied, drawing out the word with annoyance. "This is an unfortunate coincidence, that's all. You would have stayed well ahead of me if you hadn't stopped to do your... your..." She waved vaguely towards the scattering of leaves on the pavement. "Tree assault," she finally finished.

"Well, I'm going to move on now, so why don't you try keeping your distance this time?" Joel suggested tautly. "Neither of us would want any more unfortunate coincidences to happen again, now would we?"

He made a shooing motion with his hands before continuing along the street. He didn't look back, but he knew that Maggie had waited for a good count of ten before she began walking, too.

And so they walked a mile and a half to the carnival—alone, together.

FIVE

Ticket Guy

THE SCENT OF hot buttered popcorn and cotton candy floated through the carnival. Neon lights from the rides and stalls lit up the night sky, and the tuneful sounds of games and merriment played on a loop in the most comforting of ways.

Comforting to Joel, anyway. The carnival was home to him. It was his kingdom, and he and Evan were the princes. After all, they'd practically grown up there, playing in The Incredible Psychic Madam Emerald's fortune telling tent, helping Quite Old Aunt Ruby run the night shift, and selling tickets for Alleged Aunt Topaz's tarot card readings when they were barely tall enough to reach the fence. And then, when all the carnival-goers had gone home and the lights and music began to shut down, Joel and Evan would race along the train tracks in the Haunted House in the pitch black until their pulses were beating so fast they felt as though their hearts would burst.

Maximus hadn't been around back then, Joel remembered as he took his usual post selling tickets at the Haunted House, waiting for the customers to roll in. It wasn't long after their mother had left, and Maximus had spent years searching for her. He'd taken Ainsley, who was only a toddler at the time, and left eight-year-old Joel and nine-year-old Evan under the care of the alleged aunts. The aunts weren't exactly maternal, so Evan and Joel decided to take care of each other. And they'd gotten pretty good at it, too. That was, until Maximus had come back and ruined it all.

Why did he come back? Joel wondered bitterly. *He should have left with her. Evan and me, we would have been just fine without him.*

"Hey," said a voice, interrupting his thoughts.

Joel inhaled a sharp breath, startled by the presence of a teenaged boy and girl approaching the metal gate where he sat, perched on top of the railing.

His first customers of the night.

"Two tickets," the boy said cockily, slinging his arm around his redheaded girlfriend's shoulders in a lazy, possessive sort of way.

Joel unzipped the money pouch that was tied loosely around his hips and drew out a roll of tickets. He tore off two stubs and handed them to the boy in exchange for the cash.

Joel was aware of the girl's eyes travelling over him—and so, it seemed, was her boyfriend. Flinching at the affront, the boy drew his girlfriend closer, trying to recapture her gaze, but her focus stayed on Joel as he unhooked the rope barrier and gestured for them to take a seat on the train.

Blushing, the redhead thanked him profusely. Her date grimaced.

As the twosome seated themselves in a cart at the back of the train, another couple arrived. They were older, in their late thirties and wearing wedding bands. The couple laughed between themselves as they bought their tickets and boarded the train. Only once did the woman's eyes flicker to Joel. He looked away quickly.

He wouldn't have minded so much that people often took notice of him—hell, sometimes he even kind of *liked* it—but it felt like cheating somehow. It was almost like they were being tricked into noticing something different about him. Something compelling that they couldn't quite explain.

They were seeing a witch.

A trio of girls were next in the queue. They giggled infectiously as they bought their tickets and climbed aboard the train. Joel recognised them from school, but they were a few years younger than him. The energy around them was strange, Joel decided. Bright pink—not something he was used to. Most people had a dark or earthy coloured aura, with the odd one having a subtle jewel tone or, even more rarely, a warm-hued shimmer.

One of the girls let out a shriek. "You guys!" she exclaimed to her friends, leaning over her cart to where her companions occupied a two-seater. "I'm alone back here. I'm going to freak out!"

The duo in the cart ahead of her erupted into another fit of giggles.

"Why don't you ask you-know-who to sit with you?" one of them teased. "I bet he'll protect you!"

More giggles.

The solo girl leaned over the edge of her train cart and a mass of highlighted blonde curls tumbled over her shoulders. "Hey, Joel!" she called, to the obvious delight of her friends. "Wanna sit with me? I'm scared."

Joel offered her a half-smile. "You'll be fine."

She pouted back at him. "Your loss," she said, dropping back into her seat.

The trio resumed their giggling; the redheaded girlfriend kept glancing at Joel while her boyfriend vied for her attention; and the married couple buckled their safety belts before linking hands with each other.

Even though there were still five or six carts left empty, Joel pulled on the lever and the train began making its way along the tracks, gaining speed as it disappeared through the black curtains that veiled the Haunted House.

Moments later, screams of fear and cries of excitement echoed out into the carnival grounds.

Joel Tomlins smiled to himself.

He loved that sound.

MAGGIE GRAPPLED WITH her enormous stick of cotton candy, tearing off tacky pieces with her fingers and letting them dissolve on her tongue while Isla relayed the latest Kaden stories.

"I don't want to get my hopes up," Isla was saying as the two of them wandered through the carnival grounds, "but I think he might be interested in me." She broke into a nervous grin, her brown eyes wide as she waited for Maggie's reaction.

"Well, of course he's interested in you," Maggie assured her, simultaneously untangling a chunk of pink cotton candy from her sandy-blonde tresses. "I mean, why wouldn't he be?"

Isla let out a jittery breath. "You really think so? He's going to be here tonight," she said as she glanced over her shoulder into the maze of stalls and rides. "How do I look?" she asked, returning her gaze to Maggie.

Even in the dim light of the carnival, it was plain to see that Isla looked immaculate. Her flawless skin glowed and her silky black hair was pulled into a complicated braid.

Maggie gave up on trying to dislodge the sugary pink lump that was matted in her hair. "You look lovely," she assured her friend. "And you *are* lovely. He'll be crazy about you."

"But everyone wants him," Isla sighed as they weaved their way between the throngs of people. "He can have his choice of anyone in school."

Maggie resisted the urge to roll her eyes. "But *anyone* isn't you," she said obligingly.

She decided not to add that, in her opinion, Kaden wasn't all that special. Sure, he was the new guy, so that posed some novelty value. But besides that, she really didn't get what all the fuss was about. He was nice to look at, she supposed, but the guy had barely said two words to anyone all week.

Maybe that's the appeal, Maggie thought. *Brooding.*

The girls came to a stop at the ring toss stall. Absentmindedly, Isla pawed over the various prizes lined up on the table in front. She picked up a teddy bear and studied its sewn on black eyes.

"Where is he?" Isla muttered. "He has to be here somewhere."

"*Everyone's* here somewhere," Maggie pointed out. Then she took another bite of cotton candy, much to the disapproval of one of the Tomlins' family extensions who was running the ring toss booth.

"No eating around the prizes," the old woman barked, shooing the girls away from the collection of plush teddy bears and plastic water pistols.

Maggie and Isla swapped an exasperated glance before they continued walking.

"But how can I find out for sure whether he likes me or not?" Isla pressed. "How can I *really* know?"

Maggie chewed thoughtfully on her latest pinch of cotton candy. "Maybe you could just ask him," she said after she'd swallowed.

Isla's neatly arched eyebrows flew upwards in surprise. "What? Are you serious? Oh, no. I couldn't possibly..." Her thought was suddenly forgotten and she let out an excited gasp. "Ooh, Mags, look!" she exclaimed. "Let's go get our fortunes told!"

Maggie followed Isla's gaze across the crowded carnival grounds to where a purple tent had been set up. Beside it, a sign that read *The Incredible Psychic Madam Emerald* had been hammered into the earth.

Maggie pursed her lips. She recognised that stall from previous years at the carnival. "I wouldn't trust a Tomlins to tell me my fortune," she warned Isla in a hushed voice.

Isla waved her hand dismissively. "It's just for fun. Don't be so uptight." Then she grabbed Maggie's arm and started hauling her towards the little purple tent.

"Hey!" Maggie protested.

"Oh, come on," Isla laughed. "Live a little! The Tomlins family isn't that bad."

Maggie gave up and reluctantly let herself be led the rest of the way across the grounds. As they approached Madam Emerald's stall, she noticed that the fortune teller's sign had a disclaimer written in small print beneath the main lettering. *The Incredible Psychic Madam Emerald will not be held accountable for bad news. No refunds.*

"I don't like this, Isla," Maggie hissed.

But Isla had no time to reply. As if on cue, a woman poked her head out of the tent. She was large and gruff looking, with a complicated silk turban fixed atop her head and a cigarette hanging out of her mouth. She extended her arm, causing the various coins attached to her outfit to jingle.

"You haf come to find out your future," the woman rasped in a strange, unplaceable accent. "A shychic alvays knows." She tossed the half-smoked cigarette onto the ground and grinned, exposing stained yellow teeth.

Maggie wrinkled her nose. "You don't have to be psychic to figure that out," she muttered. "We're standing right outside your fortune telling tent."

The Incredible Psychic Madam Emerald made a growling noise. "*You* are not velcome," she said to Maggie. "Thee other one ish fine." She gestured for Isla to come inside.

Maggie placed one hand on her hip. "Excuse me?" she snapped. "Rude much? Why am *I* not welcome?"

"Becaush you"—the Incredible Psychic Madam Emerald waved her hand in front of Maggie—"haf something on you." She curled her top lip. "Yehs," she breathed huskily. "You cannot enter my tent. Something cleengs to you. I don't vant you bringing eet een here."

Maggie's jaw dropped. "Ex*cuse* me?" she objected. "What do you mean, something *clings* to me?" Her hand went self-consciously to the glob of cotton candy in her hair.

"There ish a spell on you," Madam Emerald explained vaguely.

Maggie's heart skipped a beat. "A *spell*? What spell?"

Madam Emerald shrugged her heavy shoulders.

"Wait, what is this?" Maggie demanded. "You just cursed me?"

Madam Emerald recoiled at the insult. "Not me! Eet ees already on you. You are curshed. Now, be gone, before eet shpreads."

"How unbelievably rude!" Maggie baulked, turning to Isla for backup.

But Isla just stood there, twiddling her thumbs anxiously.

"You," Madam Emerald went on, directing a long bejewelled finger at Isla. "Come een. You are clear. I permit you inshide." She stepped aside to allow Isla into the tent.

Isla moved to enter.

"Isla!" Maggie exclaimed, grabbing her roommate's arm. "You're just going to leave me out here?"

Isla shrugged helplessly. "Sorry, Mags, but she said you can't come in with"—she hushed her voice—"your, um, curse," she finished delicately.

Maggie stamped her foot on the hard ground. "This is an outrage! I'm a paying customer. I have rights!" She paused, then under her breath added, "Probably."

The Incredible Psychic Madam Emerald cackled. "No money een thee world ish worth a cursh." And, with that, she drew the tent curtains closed around Isla.

MAGGIE THUNDERED THROUGH the carnival towards the Haunted House. She could see Joel sitting on the metal barrier, his feet propped up on the turnstile. A small queue had formed in front of him. Mostly girls, Maggie noticed. She bypassed the line—to a few muttered complaints—and cornered Joel at the metal fence.

"What?" he asked coolly, looking down on her from his post while a chorus of shrieks rang out from inside the Haunted House.

"Your aunt, the Incredible *Psycho* Madam Emerald, won't let me have my fortune read." Maggie waved her hand wildly in the direction of Madam Emerald's tent. "And she took Isla!"

Joel peered over her head to the distant summit of the purple tent. "Okay," he said, chewing on a swizzle stick. "So?"

"*So?*" Maggie echoed loudly, flinging her arms into the air. "She was rude to me! Unthinkably rude!"

"So?" Joel repeated. "What do you expect me to do about it? She's rude to everyone."

"She told me there was something on me. She said that I was. . ." Maggie glanced furtively over her shoulder to the queue of girls behind her, then turned back to Joel. She cupped her hands around her mouth and hissed, "That I was *cursed*."

Joel cupped his hands around his mouth, too. "So?" he whispered back.

Maggie swatted his hands down. "So tell her," she fumed, her voice rising again, "to apologise! Tell her to tell me that it isn't true."

Joel tore off another bite of swizzle stick with his teeth. "I can't do that," he said simply. "If you're cursed, then I can't tell her to lie to you."

"I am *not* cursed!" Maggie exclaimed, stamping her foot.

Then she paused. Come to think of it, she *had* been experiencing a bout of bad luck lately. In fact, things had been going wrong for her all week. She'd been late to school every day; the cafeteria had sold out of cake just as she'd arrived; and she'd got an F on her Science assignment. Okay, so she hadn't really been paying that much attention in Science class, but couldn't that all be part of the curse's wicked plan, too?

"Did you curse me on Monday morning in homeroom when I took your seat?" she accused.

He looked genuinely taken aback. "No," he said. "Although maybe I should have, considering what you did to me in detention that day." His brows furrowed even now at the thought. "But if you're cursed, it's not because of me."

Maggie sighed. Granted, she hadn't exactly been on best-buddy terms with Joel lately, but she knew him well enough to spot a lie. And he wasn't lying.

She swallowed. "*Am* I cursed?" she asked Joel meekly.

Now it was his turn to cast a surreptitious glance at the queue. He turned back to Maggie, his expression suddenly serious. She stood there feebly as his gaze bore into her.

At last, he spoke again. "I can't tell. There *is* something there, though," he mused, squinting his eyes as he studied an unseen point on her shoulder. "But I can't know what it is without looking deeper."

"So look deeper," Maggie implored tersely.

Joel exhaled and wearily popped the last of his swizzle stick into his mouth. "I can't do that here. There are too many people around. You'll have to find someone else to help you."

"Who?" Maggie despaired. "It's not like I know any other . . ." She trailed off as the Haunted House train chugged through the black velvet curtain and screeched to a stop right in front of them.

Joel jumped down from the gate and gestured for the breathless passengers to disembark. Those waiting in the queue took that as their prompt to board. Maggie waited impatiently while Joel instructed the new batch of passengers on how to safely circumnavigate the Haunted House. Then he pulled on a lever and the train began along the track, disappearing from sight once more.

Maggie and Joel were alone now, surrounded by a light evening breeze that dragged the smoky scent of the carnival through the air.

Maggie bit her lower lip. "If I *am* cursed," she began again, "can you get rid of it?"

Joel shrugged. "I don't know. It depends what type of curse it is. And I wouldn't do it for free, of course."

"Fine, whatever," Maggie said, making a circling motion with her hand to hurry him along. "I'll pay you, okay? Just de-cursify me."

Joel raised an index finger. "No promises. I'll see what I can do."

Maggie let out a tense breath. "Fine." She grabbed the sleeve of his jacket. "Let's go."

"Whoa!" Joel pulled free of her. "Not *now*."

"Please?" Maggie cried. "You can't expect me to stand around cursed all night!"

"I'm working," Joel reminded her, thumbing towards the empty tracks.

"I'll pay you double!" Maggie said desperately, fumbling through her shoulder bag and stuffing a handful of notes into Joel's hands. "Here," she said. "This is all I have. Take it."

Joel stared down at the crumpled notes in his hands. "Okay," he said at last, casting a glance at the tracks. The train was nowhere in sight and the queue was still empty. "But this is just payment for a check-over," he said, stuffing the cash in his jeans pocket. "I'm going to need more if you want the curse gone. This isn't a charity case."

"Fine," agreed Maggie, once again taking hold of his sleeve and towing him in the direction of the carnival entrance. "But we've gotta move it. I'm going to have to sneak you into the dorms before Joyless starts the night shift."

"I'm not doing this at school!" Joel laughed. "You'll have to come to my house."

She stopped in her tracks, causing Joel to bump into her.

"Your house?" she echoed weakly.

"Don't act so surprised," Joel replied. "You're asking me to do a spell, aren't you? Well, where do you think I do my spells?"

Maggie shivered and wrapped her arms around herself. "You want me to hang out at the creepy old hell-pit for witches?"

"Can you stop calling it that?" he grumbled. "It's okay for me to say it, but when *you* say it, it's just offensive."

"Fine," Maggie muttered, then began walking cautiously onwards.

"And besides," Joel added as they weaved through the stalls, "you won't be *hanging out* there. You weren't invited for recreation. This is business."

They reached the main entrance, where gatherings of carnival goers were milling about. Cars were parked along the street for as far as the eye could see.

Maggie sighed. "Where are you parked?"

"Evan has the car tonight," Joel told her. "I walked, remember?"

Maggie groaned. "So how are we going to get there?" Her jade eyes paled in the moonlight. "We can't *walk*. Your house is miles away!"

"We won't have to walk," Joel answered. He scanned the street until his eyes landed on a small cherry red mini parked some ways along the pavement. "There's one," he murmured to himself.

"There's one what?" Maggie asked, following his gaze.

Joel smiled innocently. "There's one we can borrow," he said as he started towards the mini.

Maggie trotted along behind him. "What do you mean?" she called, her voice rising an octave. "Does that car belong to someone you know?"

"No. But it's easy to borrow."

"Borrow?" Maggie spluttered. "As in, *steal*?"

"Borrow as in borrow," Joel corrected, striding ahead of her. "We'll give it back."

He reached the car and tried the handle. It opened without a problem.

Maggie drew in her breath. "It wasn't locked?"

Joel smiled up at her as he slid into the driver's seat. "I have good instincts," he told her as he nodded to the seat beside him.

Wringing out her hands, Maggie crept around the car and clambered into the passenger's seat. She winced as she pulled the door shut behind her.

Inside the cold car, their breath misted the windscreen. Fuzzy dice hung from the rear view mirror and the car smelled of peppermint and perfume.

Sitting rigidly in the passenger seat, Maggie knotted her fingers together. "You should know, I've never stolen a car before. Nor do I want to be doing it now," she added, glaring pointedly at Joel.

He frowned back at her. "Would you please stop insinuating that I'm stealing this car? Because I'm *not*. I'm giving it back as soon as we're done."

"If we get pulled over, I'm telling the police you kidnapped me."

"Maybe I'll tell them *you* kidnapped *me*," Joel retorted as he familiarised himself with the dashboard.

Maggie sucked in her breath.

"Relax," Joel muttered. "We won't get caught. I have good instincts, remember?"

He found the ignition and touched his fingertip to the key slot. Then he closed his eyes and let out a slow breath.

Maggie twitched restlessly beside him. "What are you doing?" she whispered.

He opened one eye and peered at her. "I'm using my energy to start the car," he explained. "Shh." His eyelid dropped again.

Maggie folded her hands in her lap, threading and unthreading her fingers while they sat in silence.

All of a sudden, the rumble of the engine exploded to life. The car's headlamps lit up the street before them and the stereo boomed, blaring a pop song.

Maggie jumped, clutching at her heart as the new 'it' band belted out a catchy up-tempo melody.

Joel turned to her and grinned, then settled his hands on the steering wheel.

"You might want to put on your seatbelt," he advised.

Maggie readily obliged.

With that, Joel swung the car out onto the road and sped off into the night.

SIX

Something Akin to Fear

THE CAR ROCKETED through the backcountry, tearing along the narrow mountain roads while trees whizzed past on both sides.

Leaving one hand resting lightly on the steering wheel, Joel wound down the driver's side window. The rush of air whipped across his skin and through his hair.

"Hands on the steering wheel, lunatic!" Maggie cried, covering her eyes with her fingers.

This was fun. He hardly ever got to drive without Maximus or Evan breathing down his neck. Or Ainsley complaining about something. It was nice to drive alone.

"Are you trying to kill us both?"

Okay, so he wasn't alone, exactly. But it was only Maggie.

He cast a quick glance to the seat beside him and caught a glimpse of Maggie's sandy coloured hair fluttering in the open window.

"Watch where you're going!" she squealed, her own eyes still covered by her hands.

Joel swung a hard left and the car juddered over the uneven ground leading up to Really Old Aunt Pearl's house.

"Slow down!" Maggie exclaimed as they bumped up and down in their seats.

Joel laughed. "Sorry," he said, but he didn't take his foot off the accelerator. Not until they'd reached the clearing in front of the ramshackle old mansion.

He slammed his foot on the brake and they jolted forward to an abrupt stop.

Only then did Maggie lower her hands from her eyes. She immediately turned her angry glare on Joel.

He held up his palms and smiled. "Sorry," he offered again.

Taking a deep breath, Maggie turned her attention to the windscreen, through which she could see the ancient stone mansion. The old hell-pit was bathed in moonlight, making it look particularly imposing.

Joel watched her expression change from fury to fear. The glow of the energy around her shifted too, going from the hazy blue of trepidation to the dull purple of terror.

A tiny knot formed in his stomach, even though her reaction hadn't come as a surprise. After all, that's how everyone looked when they were confronted with the Witch House for the first time.

People looked at *him* that way sometimes, too. And once in a while, he even saw it in the mirror.

She knew what she was getting herself into when she accepted my help, Joel reminded himself. *She was the one who sought* me *out.*

He shook off his apprehension and stepped out of the mini. The air was colder here, and the wind howled through the clear night air. The trees shuddered as the breeze raked through them, bowing at his arrival.

Maggie climbed out of the car after him and hurried to his side. Together they paced towards the mansion.

"I hope it's nicer inside than it is outside," she muttered as they approached the front porch.

"It isn't," Joel replied.

She grimaced as she gingerly negotiated the rickety front steps.

Joel heaved open the front door and stood aside for Maggie to step through. She took her cue and trod carefully across the threshold.

As usual, it was dim in the mansion's entrance hall. Only one oil lamp had been lit to illuminate the space, and a veil of cobwebs muted its weak light. The misted glow of moonlight leaked in through the tall leaded-glass windows, casting long shadows across the staircase.

Joel took the lead, heading for the stairs. "Watch out for the third step," he said with a backwards glance. "It's not there."

"Oh," Maggie's shaky voice returned to him. "Noted."

Joel listened to the echo of their footsteps as they neared the upper hallway. If he listened carefully, he could hear the quick pounding of her heartbeat and the rasp of her nervous breath.

He wondered what she was more nervous about—the house, the spiders, or him.

Noticing a particularly large spider on the bannister, he subtly brushed it aside, just in case it was the spiders.

Once they'd reached the top of the stairs, he made for his bedroom. There were plenty of other rooms leading off the corridor, but in the weeks that the Tomlins family had been at the house, Joel had hardly explored them at all. What would have been the point? This wasn't *his* home; it was Evan's. For him, it was just a stop gap until he could bail.

Something better will come along, Joel told himself as he shouldered open his stiff bedroom door.

As Maggie followed along behind him, Joel noticed that her heartbeat began to slow, as though the room was calming her a little. Although he couldn't think of why that might be; his room was hardly a safe haven.

"So this one's yours?" she asked, standing unusually close to him as she surveyed his bedroom.

Joel nodded. He couldn't help but notice the faint aroma of her sweet scented shampoo clinging to the air.

Bubble gum, he thought, momentarily indulging in the scent before reminding himself that this was *Maggie*—and that, as a rule, he really shouldn't breathe her in.

He stepped away from her, putting some distance between them.

There, he thought defiantly. *Much better*. He inhaled a deep breath of his moth ball smelling bedroom instead.

Maggie shuffled closer to him again.

"What are you doing?" he demanded, nudging her away. "Stop standing so close to me."

She crinkled her nose and took a generous sidestep away. "Sorry, but your house is creepy."

Joel sighed. "Let's just get this over with, okay?"

"Please," Maggie said with a shudder.

There was a pause.

"So, what exactly is it that we're doing?" she asked, wrapping her arms about herself as she continued to peer curiously around Joel's bedroom.

The bed on the left was untouched and its old-fashioned floral bedspread was gathering dust. The bed on the right remained unmade in a tangle of sheets.

Joel crossed the room to a set of antique French doors and drew open the thin white drapes. He pushed out the doors and stepped onto a small rusty balcony that overlooked the surrounding forest. The full moon shone high above in the starlit sky, somehow seeming larger and brighter than it had been in town.

"Come here," Joel instructed, gesturing to the open doorway. "You need to face the moon."

Maggie pursed her lips. "Why?"

Joel met her gaze. "I don't know. Just... because."

She eyed him cagily as she edged forward to stand in the open doorway. The evening breeze whistled through the balcony railings, catching stray strands of Maggie's hair and carrying the scent to Joel.

He shivered.

"Now what?" Maggie asked, turning back to face him.

He gathered himself. "Now we begin."

Stepping up behind her, he looked out over her head into the night.

"Stay still," he said. "I need to check the—" He stopped himself before the word *spell* escaped his lips. He knew it was no secret that he was a witch, but he'd never actually performed a spell on a person before—not a girl person, anyway. "Just stay still," he finished.

He left her alone on the balcony for a moment while he retrieved his book from under the unmade bed. It was a tatty leather-bound journal, crammed with mostly hand-me-down spells and trial-and-error incantations. Every witch worth his salt had one of these. Joel had been adding to his for years, jotting down whatever spells he found useful. His wasn't as jam-packed as Maximus's or even Evan's, but it blew Ainsley's out of the water—which was good enough for Joel.

"Um, Joel?" Maggie called from the balcony doorway.

Preoccupied, he made a mumbling noise in response and continued flipping through the worn pages of his journal.

"How long do I have to stand here for?"

Joel glanced up at her. She was facing away from him, her eyes trained on the moon like he'd instructed. Her arms were at her side and she was flexing her fingers, tugging anxiously at some frayed threads on the stitching of her jeans. Her hair moved gently in the wind, tumbling down the back of her white jumper.

Joel's heart gave a strange tug.

He cleared his throat. "Not much longer," he said. He continued to leaf through the journal until he landed on a page with the handwritten heading *See Things Better.*

He smiled sentimentally at the childlike handwriting and his nine-year-old self's description of the spell.

"Okay," he called to Maggie. "I've got it."

Carrying the open book, he walked back over to where she stood. Positioning himself behind her, he carefully moved her hair aside and placed his left hand between her shoulder blades.

This feels weird, he thought. But at least she was turned away from him so she wouldn't be able to see the colour that was undoubtedly rising to his cheeks.

"This feels weird," Maggie said.

"Just hold still," he managed in reply.

With his left hand still on her back and his right hand cradling the open journal, Joel concentrated on listening to the whir of the wind outside. To the ever quickening pulse in Maggie's veins. To the distant rustle of leaves in the forest. He listened to it all.

After a few moments, he began to read aloud the words he had penned many years ago.

"*Granted sight,*

We seek in light,

Reveal, and see,

Show secrets unto me."

All of a sudden, a gold radiance surrounded Maggie like a layer of gilded armour cocooning her. Joel felt it tingle through his fingertips where he was touching her. He heard it pulsating through her, as though it had a heartbeat of its own.

It was powerful, he realised. Impenetrable. As the gold light swam around his fingertips, it made his blood rush and his eyes sting. Then Joel was thrown backwards, as if he'd been struck by lightning—lightning that emanated from Maggie herself.

The jolt sent him hurtling backwards across the room until he collided into the wall. His head clipped against the plasterboard and he dropped to the floor, dazed.

The gold glow faded and Maggie spun around in shock.

"Joel!" she cried, rushing across the room and crouching on the floor beside him. "What happened?" Her eyes widened, searching his for an explanation.

With speckled vision, he looked up at her. "Maggie," he whispered, running his hand through his hair. "You've got something on you, that's for sure."

Both her hands flew to her mouth. "A curse?" she choked out.

Joel's gaze strayed to the moon beyond the balcony. Whatever it was that was surrounding Maggie, it had enough force behind it to throw him across the room. More precisely, whatever it was didn't want him touching her. Didn't want *anything* touching her, probably.

She was private property.

Maggie grabbed hold of Joel's arm and urged his attention to return to her. "What is it?" she demanded.

He swallowed. Something akin to fear rose in his chest. How was he supposed to answer that?

"I don't know," he said at last. "But it was definitely something."

SEVEN

Horror vs. Romance

MAGGIE AND JOEL hadn't said much else to each other on Friday night after the incident on his bedroom balcony. Joel had just mumbled a few non-committal comments, before silently driving Maggie and the borrowed car back to the carnival, where they'd immediately gone their separate ways.

Now it was Sunday evening, and Blonde Lauren and Hilary were on their way to Maggie and Isla's dorm room for their customary Sunday night movie marathon. And Maggie was determined to push all thoughts of curses—and Tomlinses—to the back of her mind.

While Isla waited at the room for the others to arrive, Maggie busied herself microwaving popcorn in the boarding house kitchen. Of course Joyless would undoubtedly be patrolling the halls to enforce her strict eleven o'clock p.m. visitors curfew on the two non-residents, but the sun had only just set so they still had hours of movie time left.

Maggie hadn't told her friends about what had happened with Joel on Friday night. It wasn't that she wanted to keep it a secret—but how was she supposed to tell them that she was cursed? They'd think she was crazy. Besides, Isla had been there when the Incredible Psycho Madam Emerald had delivered the unfortunate news, and Isla had just laughed it off. And now Maggie was beginning to feel like she should laugh it off, too.

So why couldn't she?

The memory of Joel being thrown across his bedroom, and the harrowed look on his face that followed, had been playing on a loop in her mind ever since.

The microwave pinged and Maggie was jolted back to the present. She took out the jumbo-sized bag of popcorn and emptied the steaming contents into a plastic bowl, nibbling on a few pieces before leaving the kitchen.

Cradling the overflowing bowl in her arms, Maggie raced up the boarding house's spiral staircase until she reached the third floor. She nudged open her dorm room door with her foot and ducked inside. Isla had drawn the purple drapes across the leaded-glass windows and had heaped a mountain of cushions and blankets on the floor between their two beds.

Isla and Blonde Lauren were already planted in the centre of the comfy arrangement while Hilary, dressed in a plaid shirt and black skinny jeans, hovered in front of the small TV, sifting through the stack of DVDs.

"Seen it... seen it... . despise it..." Hilary muttered to herself as she methodically rifled through the movie selection.

"Hilary!" Blonde Lauren whined from her spot on the floor. "You can't veto *all* of them. I thought tonight was my choice?"

Hilary let out a pained groan. "You know I can't allow that, Lauren. You'll pick some misogynistic love story"—she made air quotes at the word *love*—"which glorifies the regression of feminism whilst fooling the sheep-herd masses into believing that it promotes equality."

Maggie opened her mouth to speak but didn't get the chance.

"—when, in fact," Hilary went on without missing a beat, "the dated gender stereotype subtext is being rammed down our throats from the opening credits."

Maggie closed her mouth and Blonde Lauren pouted.

Isla smiled. "Ooh, that sounds good! I'm definitely in the mood for a rom-com tonight."

Hilary scowled at her. "I mean, just look at this!" she continued her rant as she waved a DVD case in front of their faces.

A glamorous platinum-haired actress smirked back at them from the plastic box, her lips pink and glossy and her porcelain face air-brushed to perfection. A slinky scarlet dress clung to her curvaceous frame and, captured in the still-frame behind her, the leading male ogled with wide-eyed wonder.

"Vile," Hilary declared, tossing the DVD box onto the floor. "And just think—this is the so-called modern society we live in."

"Hey!" Blonde Lauren protested as she scrambled across the mound of cushions to retrieve the DVD. "I want to watch this one," she said, clutching the movie protectively to her chest. "The reviews on watch-rom-com.com say it's the movie of the decade."

"Brainwashed," Hilary uttered. "Sometimes I worry about you, Lauren. You'll believe anything that anyone tells you, no matter how far-fetched it is."

Blonde Lauren scowled. "That's not— "

All of a sudden, Maggie couldn't stand it anymore. She jumped to her feet, tipping the bowl of popcorn in the process.

"I'm cursed!" she declared, covering her eyes piteously. When she peeped out through her fingers, she saw three blank faces staring back at her.

Isla's expression crumpled into laughter. "Not this again! Come on, Mags, you're not seriously still freaked out about what Madam Emerald said, are you?"

Maggie dropped her hands and pressed her palms together anxiously. "Well, yes, actually, I kind of am," she admitted.

Isla laughed again. "The Incredible Psychic Madam Emerald wouldn't let Maggie have her fortune told," she explained to the other girls. "And now Maggie thinks she's cursed."

Maggie placed her hands on her hips. "It's not like I jumped to that conclusion on my own, Isla. Madam Emerald *told* me herself that I was cursed! And then Joel said it, too," she mumbled quietly.

"Joel Tomlins?" Hilary spluttered. Her heavily made-up eyes widened behind her chunky red fashion glasses.

Isla groaned. "Of course he's going to tell you that. You guys bicker all the time," she pointed out. "He'd say anything to get a rise out of you."

"He's cute, though," Blonde Lauren added. "You know, for a. . ."

"W-i-t-c-h," Maggie spelled out.

Blonde Lauren shifted in discomfort.

"You're not cursed, Maggie," Isla assured her as she neatly scooped the spilled popcorn back into the bowl.

Outside, the wind howled as it swept through the trees, rattling the window pane.

Blonde Lauren gave an audible shudder. "Can we quit talking about curses, please? It's giving me the creeps."

"Tell me about it!" Maggie exclaimed. "You're not even the one who's cursed. So how do you think *I* feel?"

"It's not real!" Isla giggled. "You can't believe a thing those so-called witches say. For example, wanna know what Madam Emerald told *me*?" She continued on hurriedly, looking excitedly between the other girls without waiting for a response. "She said that Kaden wasn't interested in dating me, and then look what happened—we ended up hanging out together all night after Maggie ditched me." Isla smiled coyly at the memory.

"Ooh, really?" Blonde Lauren's eyes lit up with the promise of a more appealing topic of discussion.

Isla nodded. "Madam Emerald is a hack," she went on, tucking a strand of silky black hair behind her ear. "And Joel is. . . Joel."

Maggie sank back down to the floor. Maybe Isla was right. Maybe this was Joel's payback for the stunt she'd pulled in Joyless's detention dungeon.

But still, why couldn't she forget the look on his face that night at his house? Why couldn't she shake the feeling that this was more than a joke?

As the other girls resumed the movie debate over horror vs romance, Maggie found herself replaying the events of Friday night in her mind. It didn't matter how many people told her otherwise—she couldn't erase one cold, hard fact: Joel had been scared.

And now, so was she.

EIGHT

Young Guy, Lamborghini

WHEN THE FINAL school bell rang at the end of the afternoon, Maggie was up and out of her seat before it had even finished its chime. As her classmates' chairs scraped against the floor, echoing off the high ceilings, Maggie was already hurrying across the classroom. She angled herself in the doorway, forcing people to manoeuver around her as she crossed her arms and stared in Joel's direction. She noticed a weary expression creep onto his face as he realised that he couldn't avoid her this time.

It was already Tuesday, and he had managed to sidestep her for two whole school days—not to mention the entire weekend.

Joel was the last one remaining in the classroom. Finally, he got up from his desk and began to tentatively approach the door, doing his best to avoid her gaze.

Maggie held her ground in the middle of the doorway. "Well?" she pressed before he had a chance to say anything.

"I'm thinking," Joel told her.

Maggie let out an incensed groan. "You've had four days to think!" she cried. "Haven't you come up with anything yet?"

"Nope." Joel eased past her and began down the mosaic-tiled corridor.

Maggie stormed after him. "Joel!" she called, exasperated. "I thought you were going to help me?"

"I'm trying," he replied, barely glancing over his shoulder.

Maggie grabbed the back of his T-shirt, forcing him to stop walking. Begrudgingly, he turned around to face her.

"Try harder," she snapped. "I'll pay you. I'll do anything. I just have to get rid of this . . . this curse thing." Her face was taken over with an expression of revulsion as she said the last few words.

Joel raked his hands through his hair. "I've told you already —I'm thinking."

"But it's been four days!" Maggie wailed, stamping her foot on the highly polished floor.

A couple of students passing through the corridor raised their eyebrows at the scene. She shot them a sour look and they scuttled past.

Maggie took hold of Joel's elbow and steered him towards a discreet alcove. "Bad things have been happening to me, Joel," she whispered. "Cursey things."

He frowned. "Like what?"

"Ms Joyless is on my case all the time—"

Joel snorted. "Oh, well, if *that's* your reasoning, then everyone is cursed."

"And I keep losing things," Maggie went on, ignoring him. "My homework, my clothes. . ."

Joel's gaze wandered down to her peach coloured t-shirt.

Maggie folded her arms across her chest. "Not while I'm *wearing* them," she said, flustered. "They disappear from my room."

"Oh." Joel shifted the weight of his gym bag on his shoulder. "So there's a kleptomaniac on the loose," he guessed.

Maggie grimaced. "There's a curse on the loose, more like." She took a step towards him and lowered her voice. "Not on the loose. On the *me*."

Joel sighed. "Okay, so you've got a spell on you," he agreed. "But *I* don't know what it is, either. And it's not necessarily what you think it's going to be, so until I figure out exactly what it is we're dealing with, there's not a whole lot I can do about it."

Maggie let out a strangled noise, attracting more prying gazes from passers-by. "But you're not even *trying* to figure it out," she complained.

"I'm thinking about it," Joel repeated calmly.

"You've been avoiding me for four days!" she accused.

"I'm thinking about it from afar."

Maggie slapped her hand to her forehead. "Communicate, Joel," she grumbled. "Geesh. I'm freaking out over here, and the only person I know who can help me is you. And you're not being very helpful."

"I'm helping," Joel protested. "I'm here, aren't I?"

Maggie gave a reluctant nod. "Yeah, I guess." Then she brightened. "Does that mean we can go somewhere and talk about it?"

Joel's eyes narrowed. "I thought we just *did* talk about it."

Maggie deflated again.

"I can't talk about it now, anyway," Joel added. "I've been picked for the soccer team and I've got to get to practice. I'll talk to you tomorrow." He turned and continued along the corridor.

"Can I at least get your number?" Maggie yelled after him.

"No," he replied without looking back.

A few girls lingering at their lockers stifled giggles. Maggie cringed. This was utterly humiliating.

Joel Tomlins is evil, she fumed silently. *And he's going to help me whether he wants to or not.*

Flipping her hair over her shoulder, she marched towards the boys changing rooms. Beside the door through which Joel had just disappeared stood Charlie Wells, whose head was dipped over a stream of water coming from the drinking fountain.

With a deep breath, Maggie approached. "Hi, Charlie," she said brightly.

Charlie's thumb slipped from the button and the stream of water immediately disappeared. He looked up, wiping droplets from his mouth.

"Yo, Ellmes," he said with a lazy grin. "To what do I owe the pleasure?"

Maggie winced. Generally she and Charlie didn't socialise —and she wasn't in any hurry to change that.

"Can I borrow your phone?" she asked in the sweetest voice she could manage. "I've lost mine and I need to send a text." She forced a smile.

Charlie puffed out his already enormous chest. "Anything for a chick in distress," he said as he slid his touchscreen from his varsity jacket pocket. "Dictate, sweet thang."

Maggie fought back the urge to retch. "Can I type it?" She tried out an eyelash flutter, emulating how she'd seen Isla do it for guys she liked.

Charlie straightened in concern. "What's wrong with your eyes, dude?"

Maggie stopped fluttering. "Can you just give me the phone?" she grumbled. "It's private."

Charlie grinned. "You can tell me anything," he said, sidling a little closer to her. "C-dog can keep a secret." He winked.

Ugh, thought Maggie. *He calls himself C-dog?*

"It's *really* private," she insisted. "Girl stuff, you know?"

He took a step back. "Oh," he exhaled, then thrust his phone into her hands like it was about to detonate. "Girl stuff," he echoed with a shudder. "Right."

She snatched the phone and quickly scrolled through his contacts list. She found Joel's name and selected the option to send his number as a text message. Then she hastily typed her own number into the recipient box and pressed send. A moment later, her phone beeped from inside her shoulder bag.

Charlie frowned. "Hey, was that your phone?" he asked, staring down at her bag.

"No," Maggie lied, laughing lightly. "No, it was my... Bye!"

Then she hurried away in case he decided to check his outbox.

THAT EVENING AFTER soccer practice, Joel took his time in the locker room. It was days like this that he wished he lived on campus. He didn't want to go home. And if he stuck around the school long enough, maybe he wouldn't have to.

In fact, considering all the people Joel was avoiding at the moment, he was running out of places he could hide. At the house, he was tired of watching Maximus mould Evan into the family's saviour; the super witch whose sole purpose was to bring glory to the Tomlins coven. That wasn't Evan. Or, at least, it *hadn't* been.

And then, of course, there was Maggie . . . It wasn't that Joel didn't *want* to help Maggie, just that he really didn't know how to. This was serious witchcraft, and he was out of his depth.

So, instead, he hid.

After the rest of the team had showered and left, Joel lay on one of the locker room benches and stared up at the generic grey ceiling. Droplets of humidity from the shower stalls clung to the lights, threatening to drip down and splatter on the tiled floor.

The locker room door opened.

"Joel?" came a voice he knew.

Joel rolled onto his side and greeted Evan with a tentative smile.

"Hey," he said.

"Hey," Evan replied. "What are you doing? All the other guys have left already. I saw Charlie on his way out and he said you were still in here—"

"You don't have to come to my practices, Evan," Joel told him.

Evan walked across the room and, shoving Joel's feet off the end of the bench, took a seat beside his brother.

"I know," he said. "But I want to. I like watching you guys play, even if it's just a warm up. And even if you do suck."

Joel grinned and gave his brother a playful kick.

"So, are you planning on sleeping here tonight?" Evan asked lightly, peering down at his brother.

Joel sat up from his supine position. "Do you think anyone would notice?"

"*I'd* notice. So would Ainsley, and Pippin." Evan turned his gaze to the row of lockers. "And Dad," he finished.

Joel snorted. "I'm sure you'd all survive without me."

"I wouldn't."

Joel stayed silent and followed his brother's lead, staring at the bank of metal lockers in front of him.

Evan cleared his throat. "So," he started, "are you ready to go or what?"

Joel covered his face with his hands and lay back down on the bench.

"What's wrong?" Evan asked wearily. "Tell me, Joel."

Joel groaned. "Nothing's wrong," he said, unable to meet his brother's gaze. The truth was, he didn't know where to begin. Ever since they'd moved into Really Old Aunt Pearl's house, life as they'd known it had changed. And it just kept changing. "I'm just . . . tired."

"Tired of what?" Evan pushed. "The house? Dad?" He looked to his sneakers. "Me?"

"No," Joel answered, sitting up again. "Not you. I'm just..."

"Tired?" Evan guessed.

Joel nodded his head, fixing his eyes on the bank of lockers again.

Evan patted him on the shoulder before standing up. "Come on," he said, walking towards the door. "I'm hungry. We could get chili fries on the way home."

Joel's stomach rumbled at the mention of greasy food. *Damn Evan. He knows my willpower isn't strong enough to say no to that.*

Wearily, Joel rose to his feet and stretched his arms over his head. "Make it a cheeseburger and you're on," he bartered.

"Done," said Evan.

Joel slung his gym bag over his shoulder and set off after his brother. Just the two of them.

Just like old times, he thought, smiling to himself.

They walked through the deserted annex and out into the night. The Jeep was one of the only cars left in the parking lot. Evan jumped into the driver's seat and started the engine while Joel climbed into the passenger seat.

They began heading off campus, driving towards the main road.

"You guys played okay today," Evan said as he steered into a steady flow of traffic.

Joel began fiddling with the dial on the radio. "But did you see Charlie miss that shot?"

Evan smiled. "Yeah. He sucks."

"Mm-hmm," Joel agreed. "How do you think I did?" His voice betrayed him, giving way to a tremor on the final word. He kept his focus on tuning the stereo, trying to pretend he didn't care about the answer.

"Good," Evan replied, his eyes trained on the road. "Really good. I mean, you've got some bad habits, but it's nothing a little training won't fix."

Joel sat back in his seat. "Yeah," he accepted. "I can work on bad habits." He hesitated and traced the stitching on his jeans with his thumbnail. "How's your, um, *training* going?"

Evan stiffened. This was a subject the brothers didn't really talk about anymore. Not since they'd stopped doing spells together and Maximus had taken over Evan's training, bringing it to a whole other level.

"It's going okay," Evan said at last.

Joel stared at his hands. "Yeah? So, is it. . . different?"

"Kind of." Evan's voice was tense.

Gated houses whizzed past the Jeep's windows as they cruised leisurely down the suburban road.

"Different how?" Joel asked, his voice sounding tinny in his ears—reminding him of how he was now an outsider in something that he and Evan used to share.

"Well," Evan started, fidgeting with the steering wheel, "the spells are stronger, for one."

"Oh, yeah?" Joel looked over at his brother now.

Evan nodded. "You know when you do a real heavy incantation and it just completely rocks you?" he asked, beginning to speak more fluidly now.

Joel nodded. He loved that feeling.

"It's kind of like that," Evan continued, "but bigger. *Much* bigger. It feels as though your body is going to implode, but it also feels. . ."

"Good?" Joel finished for him.

Evan nodded his head and grinned.

Joel couldn't help but want to know more. After all, the spells Evan was doing were at a calibre Joel had never known—and perhaps never would.

"So, is it like that time we did one of Dad's locating spells?" he asked. "That dark one that made us sick for days?"

Evan thought about it for a moment. "Sort of, in some ways," he agreed distantly. "But it's better. And I know I'm capable of controlling it now." He flashed another grin.

Joel kicked idly at the dash. "Must be good to be Chosen."

Evan shrugged.

"It must be," Joel surmised. He gave a low whistle. "It's weird to think that we'll never be at the same level again, isn't it?"

"We're still brothers. We're just the same."

"We're not the same."

They both fell silent, and by the time Evan steered the Jeep into the parking lot of Denver's Burger Shack, there was an awkwardness lingering between them.

Joel winced. He didn't want things to be this way between them anymore. He had to say something. *Anything*.

He opened his mouth to speak, but his brother got in first.

"Man," Evan breathed, "I forgot how much I love this place."

Joel smiled. "Yeah. What a dive."

"A lot of memories here, though," Evan added.

Joel considered it for a moment as he looked out at the roadside diner with its weather-beaten sign and grimy windows. After Maximus had left, Joel and Evan had come here nearly every night, just the two of them. Most days they couldn't afford anything more than a coke between them. But they were good memories. In fact, they were some of the happiest memories of Joel's life.

Together they left the Jeep and strode into the diner. They were immediately engulfed by the scent of fries and coffee as the thin aluminium door rattled shut behind them. It was relatively busy for a weeknight, with people lined up on stools along the counter and many of the pale blue booths already occupied.

The brothers found an empty booth at the back by the window and slid into seats opposite one another.

Evan scanned the laminated menu while Joel toyed with the salt shaker and gazed out the window at the forest beyond the parking lot. Like all the other cars, the Jeep's windscreen was gleaming with the reflection of the setting sun.

He scanned the diner, then looked back to the parking lot. "Hey," he said to Evan.

Evan looked up from the menu. "What?"

"Brunette woman, SUV. Bearded Guy, Chevy truck. Man at the Counter, silver Ford," he began, rattling off the pairings of drivers and cars. It had been a favourite game of theirs when they were younger. "Young Guy, Lamborghini—"

Evan guffawed. "Nuh-uh. No way," he disagreed, thumbing towards a rusty black Toyota parked along the forest border. "Young Guy, Toyota."

Joel placed the salt shaker down on the table and fixed his brother with a steely gaze. "No," he said defiantly. "Young Guy, Lamborghini. *Old* Guy, Toyota."

Evan raised an incredulous eyebrow and placed the menu down on the table. "No way. *Young* Guy, Toyota," he reasserted.

"Don't give me that!" said Joel, laughing. "You may be the Chosen One, but nobody—*nobody*—knows energy like I do." He offered his brother a challenging grin, not knowing how the new Evan, the *Chosen* Evan, would respond.

Evan smiled as the waitress approached. She was a stout woman in her late forties. Her bleached blonde hair was piled like a haystack at the crown of her head and she smelled strongly of floral perfume and tobacco.

"What can I get you boys today?" she asked in a husky monotone through lips that were smeared with cerise lipstick.

"Double cheeseburger with everything," Joel answered without looking at the menu. "Thanks."

She scribbled the order onto her tiny notepad. "And for you?" she asked, looking up at Evan and taking a moment to notice his striking appearance.

He gave her a beautiful smile. "Same," he said.

She tucked the pencil nub behind her ear and waddled off towards the kitchen.

Alone again, Joel and Evan returned to a safe topic of conversation—soccer. Joel watched as Evan's lilac eyes illuminated while he spoke about the day's scrimmage and recounted the plays he thought the team should run this season.

After a while, Joel found himself smiling along with his brother.

"See?" said Joel. "You miss it, don't you?"

Evan blushed.

"If you miss it, then why don't you just join the team?" Joel asked. "Coach would jump at the chance to get you back."

Evan's handsome face was red from ear to ear now. "No," he said, flustered. "I'm busy with school and . . . you know."

"Chosen One stuff?"

Evan nodded.

"So make time," Joel suggested. "You have to have *some* life outside of witchcraft, no matter what Dad might say."

Evan shook his head. "No, I can't. Besides, this is your year. It's your turn."

Joel leaned back in the booth. "Come on. I could use a challenge. Who knows? I might actually beat you."

They both laughed.

Joel's phone buzzed inside his jeans pocket. "Hold that thought," he said.

He retrieved his phone and opened his message inbox. His eyes widened when he saw the text message displayed on the screen, sent from an unknown number.

Help me. Maggie.

For a second Joel was lost for words.

"What is it?" Evan asked from across the table.

Joel re-read the message to himself. *How did she get my number?* he wondered. It wasn't as though they ran in the same circles or anything.

"Joel?" Evan prompted. "Who messaged you? And why are you smiling like that?"

Am I smiling?

Joel instantly puckered his lips into a scowl. "It's nothing," he said, stuffing the phone back into his pocket. "It's just . . ." he trailed off.

He didn't really want to tell his brother about Maggie. Evan would harp on about the dangers of exposing his powers to a non-witch, not to mention the repercussions of interfering with another witch's spell.

And he'll probably tell Dad, Joel thought.

"It's nothing," he finished.

Joel glanced out the window just as the young guy was climbing into the Lamborghini. He broke into a wide grin.

"Well, what do you know?" he said, pressing his index finger to the window pane. "Young Guy, Lamborghini."

NINE

Chemistry

MAGGIE'S FINAL LESSON on Thursday was Chemistry with Mr Hickman. As far as teachers went, Mr Hickman was kind of okay. In fact, Maggie had always thought he seemed like someone's grandpa who'd got lost on the way home from Bridge Club and somehow landed in a school where he proceeded to spend his days blowing up chemicals. His hair was snowy white, streaked with remnants of a ginger hue, and he was doughy and about as eccentric as any Chemistry teacher should be.

Another advantage of Mr Hickman's class, was that he was deaf enough to let classroom chatter slide. So naturally Maggie partnered with Isla, and generally, they chatted.

Today was no different. Maggie and Isla were stationed at their usual work bench, equipped with a glass beaker and a selection of corked test tubes. Blonde Lauren and Hilary occupied the work bench behind.

While Isla busied herself preparing the experiment, Maggie took out her phone and began idly browsing online.

"Are we going to Casey's party tomorrow?" Isla asked as she organised the test tubes in order of use.

Maggie shrugged. "I guess," she replied without enthusiasm.

Isla shot her a quizzical look. "You don't sound excited."

"I'm *not* excited," Maggie sighed, toying with the end of her ponytail. "These parties are always the same. Blah."

Blonde Lauren lunged across her work bench to join the conversation. "No way," she argued, platinum waves tumbling over the edge of the table as she leaned forward. "Casey's party is going to be..." she paused, holding up both palms to emphasize her declaration, "*uh*-mazing."

Maggie rolled her eyes, then returned her attention to her phone, scrolling mindlessly over a web page.

"Right," Hilary drawled from the seat beside Blonde Lauren. "Because the definition of amazing is watching a herd of wasted meat-heads battle to be alpha male by displaying their peacock feathers to the women-folk. Blah," she seconded Maggie.

Blonde Lauren gasped and her eyes widened in despair. "But, you are going, aren't you?"

Hilary shifted in discomfort, folding her arms across her chest. "Well, obviously," she grumbled. "It's not like there's anything else to do in Blah-heath."

Isla swivelled in her stool to face the girls. "I don't know," she mused. "Personally I'm really looking forward to it. Kaden will be there, so..." Her smile glinted in her chocolate-brown eyes.

Maggie looked up from her phone and frowned. She'd never seen Isla so taken with a guy before. Normally the boys pursued Isla, while she remained distinctly blasé. But in this instance, it seemed as though Isla was the one doing the chasing, while Kaden remained elusive.

Sounds like me and Joel, she contemplated the irony. *Only with a little less romance and a little more curse.* Joel still hadn't replied to her text message and he'd categorically avoided her all week. She snuck a quick peek across the lab to where he was seated. At that moment, he and Charlie were hunched over a sheet of paper, discussing it heatedly.

Surely there not that excited over the worksheet? Maggie wondered. She craned her neck to see the paper that had them so rapt. It looked more like a diagram of soccer strategies than a chemistry experiment. *Figures*, she thought. *If only he got this enthused about de-hexing his acquaintances.*

At the front of the classroom, Mr Hickman was mid-experiment of his own, pouring colourful liquids into a clear glass beaker and watching with glee as the concoction fizzed and foamed. He was happily prattling away to himself—or to his students, Maggie could never be sure.

"So," Isla was saying, her focus returned to the experiment as she held two half-filled test tubes at eyelevel, "we add this to this and we should get . . ." she poured both contents of the tubes into the beaker and cheered when the blend began to foam, "that!"

"Cool," said Maggie, slipping her safety goggles over her eyes. "We did it."

Isla raised a fine eyebrow. "We?"

Maggie smiled sheepishly.

"Oh!" Mr Hickman hooted from his desk. "There she blows! We have a fizzer!" Nudging his plastic goggles up onto his head, he gestured wildly towards Maggie and Isla's work bench.

All eyes turned to them, and Isla beamed with pride.

Mr Hickman returned with his best Lunatic-Grandpa smile. "Girls, would you be so kind as to tell your fellow students how you accomplished such a feat?"

Isla delicately folded her hands together on the worktop. "Of course, Mr Hickman."

While Isla dived into a detailed breakdown of their experiment, Maggie stifled a yawn and checked the browser on her phone.

Ooh, she thought, scanning a pop-up article, *Blockbuster reopening for the holidays...*

"Maggie?"

Huh? She glanced up to see Mr Hickman staring right at her, his toothy smile plastered in place.

"Miss Ellmes?" the teacher prompted.

Why is he saying my name?

"Yes?" she replied warily.

The classroom went silent. Maggie looked to Isla for back-up, but Isla merely offered an awkward smile and nodded towards the experiment, which was now foaming inside the beaker.

"Can you explain what happened when you added the hydrogen peroxide?" Mr Hickman asked.

What is *this?* Maggie almost fell off her stool. *Why is Hickman asking questions?* He wasn't supposed to ask questions! He was the one teacher she could count on to leave her in peace.

What is this school coming to? she thought, frankly incensed. *Every lesson someone's asking you something. It's ridiculously unreasonable!*

She glanced at Isla again, searching for the answer, hoping it could be telepathically conveyed… or vocally conveyed, for that matter. But Isla's pursed lips gave nothing away. Her eyes, however, darted frantically between the test tubes and the beaker.

What does that mean? Maggie panicked. *Curse my inability to mind-read!* She winced. *Curse* was the taboo word. In fact, this could very well be yet another cruel blow from the word-that-shall-not-be-named.

She sighed. "It exploded?" she guessed.

There were a few snickered around the lab and Maggie's cheeks grew hot.

Mr Hickman's enormous smile began to collapse as though someone had popped it with a pin.

"No, no," he said, patiently. "The hydrogen peroxide." He enunciated the words as though he still held hope that she might have misheard the first time. "We've been studying this for eight weeks, dear."

Eight weeks? Maggie frowned. *Has school even been running for eight weeks?*

She drew in a deep breath and took another shot at it. "Well…" She stared down at the beaker, watching the pale pink foam spill over its ridge. "This happened," she said, pointing to the foam.

Silence.

All of a sudden, her phone lit up from where it lay dormant in her lap. Maggie glanced down in time to see a text message flash across the screen. The message was from Joel and it simply read, *changed colour.*

"It changed colour!" Maggie cried.

Mr Hickman's megawatt smile pumped back up again. "Good, good! And to what colour did it change?"

Oh, good god, Maggie deflated. *This is never-ending!*

"Pink?" she guessed, based on the pinkish hue of the liquid inside the beaker.

Mr Hickman's smile began to droop again. "But, before it turned pink...?"

Maggie's nose creased. *Wait, what? When was it another colour?*

Her phone flashed again. She hastily looked down at the screen. It was a second message from Joel.

Blue, the message read.

"Blue," said Maggie.

Beside her, Isla exhaled in relief.

"Yes!" Mr Hickman cheered. "Terrific, Terrific!" Satisfied with her response, the teacher turned away and began talking to another duo about their experiment. The usual lab chatter resumed and Maggie felt herself relax. She looked across the room to Joel and smiled.

"Thank you," she mouthed.

He grinned, then returned his attention to the paper that he and Charlie had been so focused on. Maggie returned to her own work, determined to pay attention to . . . whatever it was they were supposed to be doing.

A moment later, her phone lit up again.

She checked the screen. It was from Joel.

You should pay more attention in class.

She smiled to herself and replied. *On it.*

Before she had chance to put her phone away, the message alert flashed again.

By the way, of course I'll help you.

She met Joel's eyes across the classroom and they exchanged a grin.

"Thanks," she mouthed.

"No problem," he mouthed back.

TEN

Out of the Ordinary

ON FRIDAY NIGHT Maggie trudged the streets of Blackheath towards Casey's house. She trailed dutifully behind her friends, tuning in and out of their conversations as they headed for the party.

Blonde Lauren was tottering along the suburban path in stiletto heels and a micro-mini dress, while Hilary and Isla flanked either side of her, supporting her when she wobbled. Maggie dropped a few paces behind them, texting while she walked, and only occasionally glancing up to check she wasn't heading into peril. With a curse on the loose, who knew how many lampposts she could end up walking into?

Holding her phone securely, she scanned the last text message from Joel.

It might help if we knew who had reason to cast a spell on you, the text read. *Do you have any enemies? Anyone who might be holding a grudge?*

Maggie thought about it, then texted back. *You.*

Her phone flashed with a response. *It's not me. Who else?*

Maggie glanced up to ensure she hadn't strayed from the pavement, then quickly typed a response. *I don't know. I don't annoy anyone else.*

I find that hard to believe, Joel replied. *Think, Maggie!*

So she thought some more.

A minute later, another text message came through to her phone. It was from Joel again.

Are you going to this party tonight?

A small smile tugged at the corners of her mouth. Was this a business question . . . or personal?

Yes, she replied. *I'm heading over there right now.* After a pause, she added, *Are you going?* She pressed send, and found herself holding her breath while she waited for a response.

Lame, she reprimanded herself. *It's only Joel. Why would I care if he's at a party or not? So lame.*

After what felt like a lifetime, Joel replied. *Yeah.*

A delirious grin spread across Maggie's face.

"Hey," Isla called over her shoulder, scrutinizing Maggie with a curious expression. "What are you so happy about?" Her long dark hair swayed gently in the evening breeze, glistening beneath the moonlight.

Maggie blushed and slipped her phone into her jacket pocket. "Just lame stuff," she answered, then picked up her pace to catch up with her friends.

"Well?" said Hilary as Maggie approached.

Maggie frowned. "Well, what?"

"Have you noticed, or what?" Hilary elaborated, eyeing Maggie through her thick red-framed glasses. She was dressed head to toe in black, including a miniature top hat complete with a square of black netting which curved over her brow like a veil. She was *statementing*, as she'd put it. Mourning the demise of society.

"Noticed what?" Maggie asked, her brow furrowed. "The death of society thing?"

Hilary groaned. "No," she scoffed, adjusting her tiny top hat. "Not *the death of society thing*. I'm talking about Joel."

"Joel?" Maggie felt the blood rush to her cheeks. "What about Joel?"

Isla linked her arm through Maggie's as they walked. "Hilary thinks Joel likes you, Mags," she said with a knowing smile.

"What?" Maggie's voice went up an octave. "No. Really? Why? No?" She cleared her throat, regaining her composure. "What makes you say that?"

Hilary folded her arms. "I saw him smile twice today," she said, matter-of-factly. "Both incidents occurred when he saw you."

"Ooh," Isla teased. "You made Joel smile. Joel never smiles!"

Maggie turned beet-red. "It was probably an evil smile. He's probably plotting."

"No," said Hilary. "It was dumb happiness. I know because I was distinctly disappointed. Tomlins was one of the few people I could count on to remain perpetually dour."

Blonde Lauren popped her bubble gum. "He's cute when he smiles. Actually," she's back-tracked, "he's cute when he doesn't smile, too." She winked at Maggie. "You should totally go for it."

"No!" Maggie exclaimed. "Joel? And *me*?" she laughed giddily. "Me? And *Joel*?"

They rounded the corner onto Casey's street. An unusually high volume of cars were parked along the road outside the house, and various faces from school had already spilled over onto the front lawn. Casey's parents had gone out of town for the weekend, so logically she had declared *open house.*

The girls crossed the street and made their way over the dewy lawn towards the front porch, which had been decorated with a stream of fairy lights and colourful bunting.

For a split second, Maggie wondered how it must feel to have a home, with a porch, and a lawn. She wondered how it would feel to have parents who went away for the weekend . . . and then came home. She wondered what it must feel like to have parents at all.

She swallowed hard, then defiantly pushed the thought out of her mind. She didn't need any of these things. She had a family; she had Isla.

She squeezed Isla's linked arm a little tighter, and Isla squeezed back.

Knotted together, they crossed the threshold into the house, where a modern wood-floored hallway opened out into an elegant living room. Isla led the little foursome through clusters of Blackheath High kids to an arrangement of cream sofas set up around a table of drinks and snacks.

On one of the sofas, Kaden was seated with a couple of guys from school. When he caught sight of Isla, he waved her over.

Even though Kaden had been in Blackheath for a fortnight now, Maggie had had very few encounters with him, and up close, she realised he was rather striking. He seemed like a model, with perfectly chiselled features, cool grey eyes, and jet black hair which fell without a strand out of place. He greeted them with a charming smile.

Isla sank down beside Kaden on the sofa. "Maggie, here," she gestured to the empty spot on the other side of him.

Maggie gingerly took a seat.

"So," said Isla, leaning across Kaden to include Maggie, "I don't think you guys have properly met. This is Mags, my best friend in the whole world," she gushed. "And, this . . . well, this is Kaden." Her long eyelashes swept downwards, coyly.

"Hi," said Maggie, awkwardly. "Nice to meet you."

"Maggie," Kaden spoke her name sinuously. "I've heard so much about you."

"You, too," she replied.

Kaden raised his eyebrows. "You've been talking about me?" he teased Isla. "I'm honoured."

Isla giggled and swatted at his arm. Her long, silky black hair tumbled over onto his shirt as she edged closer to him.

"I may have mentioned your name once or twice," she purred.

"Oh?" he said, his tone mesmerizing. "And what does she say about me?" The question was directed at Maggie, but his focus never left Isla.

Maggie reached over to the snack table and took a sizable handful of party mix.

Isla answered for her, giving way to another flirty giggle, "I say that you're. . . interesting."

"Interesting?" Kaden echoed in a velvet voice. "I'm glad you find me interesting, Isla." He turned to Maggie now, catching her gaze for the first time. "It really is a pleasure to meet you," he murmured. "I hope in time you'll find me *interesting*, too."

AFTER WHAT HAD felt like a very long week, Joel was ready for the weekend. He had the night off from the carnival and he was in need of some fun—and a house party seemed like a good place to start. By the time the stars were starting to come out, he was outside the old mansion, patiently waiting for his ride. As he sat on the dilapidated porch steps, he stared out at the moonlit forest. The leaves on the trees were quivering anxiously, responding to him in ways that he could not entirely understand. Responding to questions he wasn't sure he'd asked.

Behind him, he heard the front door open and then close again with a rattling thud. Footsteps crossed the porch.

Joel glanced over his shoulder. "Whoa! Don't tell me you're actually coming?"

"Of course I am," Evan said, sitting down beside Joel on the step. "I can go to parties too, can't I?"

Joel gave a snort. "The *old* Evan went to parties, but this guy"—he waved his hand in his brother's general direction—"usually prefers to spend Friday nights with Dad."

Evan pushed Joel's hand away and frowned. "Give me a break. I'm still me."

Joel shrugged. "Kind of."

"*All* of."

"If you say so," Joel muttered under his breath.

Their conversation was cut short when a red 1978 Mustang tore up the forest path and screeched to a stop in the clearing in front of the old house. Loud bass music was thumping from the car's open windows. In the driver's seat, Charlie beeped the horn.

The brothers rose to their feet and approached Charlie's car. When Joel opened the front passenger door, the music blasted out at him so loudly it made him cringe, then laugh. He slid into his seat and slammed the car door shut.

Evan was just about to climb into the back when the front door of the mansion opened again. This time, it was Maximus who stepped out onto the porch. His eyes locked on Evan and a trace of disappointment flickered across his aged face.

"Evan, my boy," Maximus called over the pounding music that was blasting from the Mustang's speakers.

"Get in, Evan," Joel hissed.

Evan hovered in the car's open door, his hand gripping the frame while an evening breeze moved through his fair hair.

"Where are you going, son?" Maximus called out to Evan. "I thought we were working tonight."

In the front passenger seat, Joel rolled his eyes.

"I... uh..." Evan stammered. "I know, but Joel... Joel and some of the guys from school are meeting up tonight..."

Charlie let out a rowdy whoop from the driver's seat.

"And..." Evan forged on, "I was hoping I could go and hang out... for a while."

Maximus looked wounded. He stood motionless on the front porch, his old brown sweater rumpling in the building gale.

"Just for an hour," Evan finished. "Then I'll come home."

"Just for an *hour?*" Joel repeated from the front seat, peering over Charlie's head to glare at his older brother. Turning back to face the windscreen, he muttered, "You're eighteen years old, Ev. If you want to go to the party, then go to the damn party."

Maximus's gaze stayed glued to Evan while he contemplated his son's proposal. "Well, okay," he finally agreed, glancing at his watch. "So, if it's nine o'clock now, I'll see you at... ten?"

Evan swallowed, then nodded his head. "Okay, Dad. No problem."

Joel shook his head in a mixture of disbelief and disapproval, but said nothing.

Evan climbed into the backseat and Charlie gave another whoop of delight as he swung the Mustang around and sped off down the wooded hill.

SEVERAL MINUTES LATER, Charlie's car was speeding down a suburban street, approaching a large double-fronted house that was lit up and teeming with people. Dozens of other cars were parked along the street and some were creeping over onto the lawn.

Charlie squeezed into a space close to the house, uncaringly blocking in an entire row of other cars. He cut the engine and offered his knuckles to the Tomlins brothers to fist bump.

"Party!" Charlie boomed before hopping out onto the pavement.

Joel and Evan followed.

"I had to," Evan told Joel ambiguously as he and Joel crossed the lawn a few paces behind Charlie.

Joel expertly sidestepped a trio of tenth class boys who were stumbling around and singing raucously. "Yeah, I know," he told his brother, equally as ambiguous.

"I don't want..." Evan began, searching for words. "I don't want it to be like this," he managed as a discarded red plastic cup got crushed beneath his foot.

Joel stopped a few feet from the party house's front door and looked up. "It doesn't have to be," he replied emphatically. "You can tell him no. Just tell him you want to go to a goddamn party once in a while. Hell, tell him you want to play on a sports team or hang out with your friends. You need a life, Evan. Everyone misses you." He swallowed hard and shuffled his feet on the grass. "*I* miss you."

Evan's teeth clenched. "I miss you, too," he said quietly.

The brothers started walking again, climbing the front steps up to a breezy veranda with tasteful seasonal planters.

"But Dad needs me. He's got a lot riding on this," Evan continued, lowering his voice as they made their way towards the crowded entrance. "I'm the Chosen One, as you keep reminding me. I'm going to make a name for our family. I'm going to put us on the map."

Despite the tense mood between them, Joel couldn't help but laugh. He relaxed a little. "Whatever, Chosen One," he mocked. "Just enjoy your one hour of freedom, okay?"

They crossed the threshold into the house and a chorus of cheers erupted.

"Tomlins!"

"Mr T, long time no see!"

"Tomlins-o!"

Knowing that he wasn't the Tomlins that everyone was so excited to see, Joel sidestepped away from his brother and navigated his way towards the large open-plan family room, which was already packed with people from his school. It was a standard Friday night—a standard party at some standard faceless kid's house. Nothing out of the ordinary.

But then something out of the ordinary happened. From the moment Joel stepped into the living room, it was as though he'd triggered a trip switch inside of himself. He felt a tremor move through him and, just for a second, time seemed to slow down. His eyes were drawn across the room, where they landed on Maggie.

His mouth went dry and he blinked, trying to make sense of the woolly feeling inside his head. Voices now sounded muffled to him, and the people who had just seconds earlier been dancing wildly to an up-tempo beat seemed suddenly to be slowly plodding along.

Joel blinked again. *What's happening to me?*

Time had never moved like this for him before. It wasn't something he could manipulate; even Evan couldn't slow the passage of time—as far as Joel knew, anyway.

Dazed, he looked through the slow-motioned crowd, his eyes never straying far from Maggie, who was busy talking to a girlfriend with animated hand gestures.

He raked his hand through his messy brown hair. There had to be an explanation for this. For all of this.

Then, as if overcorrecting itself, everything sped up, double the speed it should have been. Voices grew louder and people darted around him in blurs. He cowered against the wall and squeezed his eyes shut.

When he opened them again, everything was back to normal.

With his heart racing, Joel looked up at Maggie again. She was looking back at him this time, and she smiled.

Joel turned away.

NEARLY AN HOUR passed before Joel could shake off the strange time-bending experience that had occurred upon his arrival. Now he was standing casually with Charlie, Evan, and some of the guys from the soccer team. They had been stationed at the wide wooden staircase for some time, leaning against the banister while Charlie entertained them with crass tales from parties past.

Joel was only half listening. His focus, though discreet, was on Maggie. From where he stood, he could just barely see her face. She was still in the open-plan family room, seated on the cream coloured couch and surrounded by various classmates.

Kaden, Blackheath High's newest arrival, had been sitting beside her for a while now. He appeared to be holding court in the living room, confident and at ease with his name-brand clothes and immaculately styled raven black hair.

The polar opposite of me, Joel thought, wishing he'd gotten his hair cut already.

Maggie appeared coolly aloof—almost indifferent—as she listened and nodded along with the conversation. Her hair was down in loose sandy blonde waves, and her lips were a pretty pink colour. Of course Joel tried not to look too closely, but somehow she was always present to him, always in his peripheral.

He looked down at his hands, disheartened to see the murky green aura of jealousy lingering on his skin. He clenched his fists and blinked until it disappeared.

Get a grip, he scolded himself, nearly laughing out loud at the idea that Maggie Ellmes was making him jealous. Or, more to the point, that the new guy who had her attention was making him jealous.

I've spent most of this week going to extreme measures to avoid her attention, he reminded himself. *That time jump must have seriously messed with my head.*

He rubbed his brow.

"Well," Evan spoke up between Charlie's anecdotes. "I guess I should bale."

Joel looked up, rejoining the conversation now. "It's still early," he said, trying to disguise the note of disappointment in his voice. "Can't you stay a little longer?"

"It's already ten," Evan replied.

Charlie flung his arm sloppily around Evan's broad shoulders, sloshing unidentified liquid from his disposable cup onto the highly polished—and very expensive—engineered hardwood flooring.

"Don't go, man," Charlie urged. "The ratio of dudes to chicks here is . . . like"—Charlie paused to let out a puff of breath as he attempted to do mental math—"well, it's like way in our favour."

Evan and Joel swapped a tired grin.

"Besides, I need a wingman," Charlie griped to Evan. "Your bro's no good to me anymore, E-dog."

"Hey!" Joel exclaimed. "Why am I no good to you?"

Charlie groaned. "Because you're all drunk on Maggie Ellmes."

Joel felt himself turn red. Clearly his focus on Maggie all night had not been as subtle as he had hoped. "What?" he spluttered. "I am not!"

Evan studied Joel with intrigue. "You didn't tell me you had a girlfriend," he said, sounding hurt. His gaze travelled the room and landed on Maggie, who was still engaged in discussion with Kaden.

"That's because I *don't* have a girlfriend," Joel replied curtly. "Especially not Maggie. I spend most of my time avoiding that girl!"

Charlie guffawed. "Whatever, dude. You want her, a-anyway," he hiccupped. "C-dog can tell. You're always, like, looking at each other and stuff."

Joel cringed. "There's nothing going on between me and..." He hushed his voice. "Maggie Ellmes," he finished furtively.

Charlie snorted. "*Right*," he answered, drawing out the word with a wink.

Joel stared daggers at him. "There isn't."

"You give each other puppy eyes all day, and you won't even look at other girls," Charlie slurred in a loud voice. "Haven't you even noticed how many girls have come up to you in the past hour alone?" Charlie shook his head and wiped a dribble of drool from the side of his mouth. "You're wasting precious moments as a guy."

"And you're just wasted," Joel shot back.

In truth, he hadn't noticed any girls approach him. He adjusted his gaze beyond his group of friends and caught sight of a few female smiles directed his way.

Growing more flushed by the second, Joel quickly returned his focus to the guys. "Shut up," he mumbled.

Evan patted him on the shoulder. "This is all very informative," he teased, "and I'd love to hear more. But I've really got to go." He climbed over the banister to get past Charlie's large build.

"What, so you're going to walk home?" Joel called after him.

"Yeah," said Evan. He smiled and glanced at Charlie, who was taking another giant slurp from his plastic cup. "And it looks like you'll be walking home too, if that's your ride." He grinned and began towards the front door.

"Anyway," Charlie went on, jabbing Joel in the ribs, "I think your girlfriend's found someone new... in the form of New Guy. You should move on, man," he advised with a booming chortle.

With Evan's departure all but forgotten, Joel glanced surreptitiously to the sofa where Maggie was seated. Kaden was leaning close to her, and as they talked she listened with interest. *Real* interest now, not the fake kind he'd seen on her face before.

Joel's heart gave a thud.

Stop it, he quickly reprimanded himself. He drew in a sharp breath and forced a smile, then tore his gaze away. *Look somewhere else*, he ordered himself. *Anywhere else.*

His eyes landed on a cheerleader named Lexi.

He smiled at Lexi and she fluttered her eyelashes back at him. Without missing a beat, she was railroading across the room towards him.

Charlie gave a wolf whistle as she approached.

"Hi, Joel," Cheerleader Lexi purred once she was close enough. She leaned against the banister just inches away from Joel, her sleek red hair falling like a curtain around them.

"Hi," he replied.

Inadvertently, his eyes flickered over to Maggie. To his surprise, she was looking back at him over Kaden's shoulder.

Good, thought Joel with a self-satisfied smile. *I want her to see. I want her to know I don't care.* He forced his gaze back to Cheerleader Lexi.

"I've been wondering when you'd notice me," Lexi said in a sultry voice.

Joel's gaze flickered back to Maggie. She was still watching.

Good, he thought again.

"Mmm-hmm," Joel managed a distracted response to Cheerleader Lexi's flirtations. The truth was, he hadn't even heard what she'd said to him. Had she asked him a question? All he could think about was wanting Maggie to feel how *he'd* felt when he'd seen her with Kaden.

Kaden, he thought with a grimace. *What a dumb name. And dumb hair.*

Cheerleader Lexi spoke once more.

Again, Joel didn't hear her.

"Yeah," he answered, preoccupied. All he could think about was how letting Maggie see him with another girl felt . . . good.

And just as he was contemplating his successful attempt at making Maggie jealous, Lexi rose to her tip toes and pressed her lips to his. Charlie and the others started cheering.

For a second, Joel was stunned. He was nearly choking on a rush of Cheerleader Lexi's overpowering pomegranate perfume before he even realised that she was kissing him.

In shock, he jumped backwards, landing on Charlie's foot and knocking the cup of unidentified liquid out of his hand. Whatever he'd been drinking spilled down the back of Joel's t-shirt.

"Damn it, Tomlins," Charlie muttered, licking the spilled drink from his thumb. But Joel hardly noticed the mess he'd created. He was too busy wiping his mouth with the back of his hand.

"No," Joel stuttered. "I'm sorry, Lexi, but. . . no."

Her pretty face contracted into a scowl.

She said something else to him, but Joel's attention had already shifted—just in time to see Maggie striding through the hallway towards the front door, leaving Kaden alone on the sofa.

Maggie cast a fleeting glance Joel's way, showing him in one simple look that she was hurt. Suddenly, his clever plan didn't seem so clever after all. He didn't feel good anymore. In fact, as he watched Maggie stumble from the house, he felt categorically and unforgivably *bad*.

ELEVEN

Pippin, Popcorn, Pots, & Pain

JOEL HAD WOKEN up early on Saturday morning, heavy with the shame of the night before. As the hours passed, he half expected Maggie to call him and yell at him or something. But she made no contact.

So, Joel went about his day as normal. He made breakfast—scrambled eggs for Ainsley and Pippin, toast for himself—but he had no appetite. He just stared at his plate, watching the butter melt into the toasted bread. His stomach was too knotted to eat.

Maximus and Evan were nowhere to be seen, presumably out working on some new spell or another. When Alleged Aunt Topaz arrived to look after Pippin, however, the self-proclaimed fortune teller for the people of Blackheath informed Joel that the plan had changed; she'd come to pick up Ainsley instead to assist her with a private palm reading session scheduled for that morning. When Joel protested that he needed Ainsley to help him look after Pippin, Topaz wouldn't hear of it. She referred to the thirteen-year-old as her lucky charm, which made Ainsley smile broadly as she hurried him out to the appointment.

"I guess it's just you and me then, Pip," Joel said to his younger brother as the front door slammed shut, kicking up a cloud of dust in its wake.

For the first time since moving into Really Old Aunt Pearl's house, Joel resolved that he should make an attempt at cleaning. He decided to start with the kitchen, since it seemed like that would be the most prudent step.

Alone in the kitchen now, Joel sat Pippin in a particularly large pot on the counter to keep him out of harm's way while the cleaning took place.

Joel tirelessly dug through the antique cabinets, discarding hoards of random old junk. He dusted the kitchen's brass fixtures and washed the crockery. He scrubbed the floor and surfaces, and even swept the dust off the grandiose chandelier that was suspended above the huge rectangular kitchen table.

Once he was finished, Joel stood back and admired his work.

He turned to his little brother, who still remained contently in the industrial-sized pot. "What do you think, Pippin?" he asked, hoping that Pippin might make a real sentence this time.

"Think, Pippin," echoed Pippin with an enthusiastic nod. Angelic blonde curls bounced into his curious violet eyes.

Joel smiled acceptingly and lifted the boy from the soup pot. "Yeah," he said, sitting him on the clean kitchen counter. "I had a feeling you'd say that."

Pippin linked his chubby fingers through Joel's and smiled devotedly at his older brother. Joel snuck a glance at his cell phone. No new messages.

"So, what do you want to do now, Pip?" Joel asked. "I've got about"—he glanced down at his watch—"an hour before my shift at the carnival starts."

Pippin's wide lavender eyes blinked hopefully back up at him.

"We could play outside," Joel suggested. "Or do you want me to take you out for ice cream?"

Pippin continued to smile and blink.

"Ice cream it is," Joel decided.

He moved to lift Pippin down from the counter just as a small piece of plastering crumbled away from the ceiling. It clipped Joel's head as it dropped to the clean floor.

Joel rubbed the sore spot on his head and frowned up at the ceiling. "Ouch," he muttered.

Pippin reached out and pressed his plump hand to Joel's chest, where his heart was beating steadily beneath his t-shirt.

"Ouch," said Pippin.

BY SIX O'CLOCK on Saturday evening, the carnival was already in full swing. The sky was darkening and the rides and stalls were lit up with neon lights. Music and chatter filled the air, and the ubiquitous carnival scent of doughnuts and popcorn wafted on the breeze.

Joel sat on the railing in front of the Haunted House, watching the queue of people form as they waited for their turn to embark the train. Cheerleader Lexi and some of her friends—who had already been on the ride twice that day—were now queuing up for the third time. Joel tried not to look at them as they giggled and tottered about in their high heels.

"Joel," the gaggle of high-pitched voices heckled him. "Oh, Jo-el!" They drew out his name as if they were calling a dog.

He kept his head down, pretending he couldn't hear. Their auras were a deep, vibrant red—powerful, competitive, and seductive.

The train chugged through the black curtains and rolled to a stop in front of Joel's post. One by one, smiling customers with flushed faces hopped out, and those waiting in the queue stepped forward to take their turns. First in was a middle-aged couple; then a group of younger boys; then came a family. The last ones to board were the girls in Lexi's clique.

"We've been calling you," Lexi purred as she leaned forward to take her ticket.

Joel shrank back.

"Yeah, Joel," one of the other girls baited him. "Didn't you hear us?" The whole tribe erupted into giggles.

Joel stood rigid as he handed them their tickets. He glanced towards the train, where the other riders were strapping themselves into carts.

"Listen, Lexi," he said, cringing as the onlookers virtually salivated at getting to witness the exchange. "I'm sorry about last night—"

"That's fine," she replied in a sultry voice. "We can try again tonight."

Joel stepped back until he was pressed against the cold metal railing. "No, Lexi," he said. "I shouldn't have kissed you. There's. . . someone else."

Her hazel eyes darkened. "What do you mean? Like, you have a girlfriend?" she challenged.

Joel bristled. "She's not my girlfriend," he said defensively. "I just. . . I like her."

As he spoke the words aloud, no one was more shocked to hear the confession than Joel himself.

Oh, god, he thought, heavy all of a sudden. *It's true. I like Maggie.*

"Who is she?" Lexi demanded, folding her arms and glowering.

From the corner of his eye, Joel noticed the hecklers glowering, too.

"No one you know," he answered.

Lexi let out a taut breath, then rifled through her purse. She pulled out an eyeliner pencil and snatched up Joel's hand, then scribbled something onto his palm.

"There," she said. "If it doesn't work out with your *girlfriend*, you know who to call." She winked and sauntered to the train, flanked by her doting cheerleader army.

Joel pressed his hand to his brow, unsure of what had just happened. He waited for the girls to climb into their carts before he hastily pulled the lever. The train lurched to life and disappeared into the dark chasms of the Haunted House.

He let out a breath.

Across the carnival grounds, Joel saw Ainsley strolling through the crowd towards him, cradling a giant bucket of popcorn.

"Is that dinner?" Joel asked as Ainsley approached. He reached out for a fistful of popcorn as soon as Ainsley was close enough.

Ainsley hugged the bucket tightly to his chest. "*My* dinner," he corrected, his blonde curls lit up by the lights of the Haunted House. "Aunt Toppy bought it for me."

"Figures," Joel muttered, rolling his eyes at his brother's affectionate term for Alleged Aunt Topaz. "And where *is* this favourite aunt of yours?"

Ainsley stuffed a handful of popcorn into his mouth. "She's helping the Incredible Psychic Madam Emerald," he garbled.

"And Evan and Dad?" Joel asked.

"Where do you think?" Ainsley replied wryly, giving Joel a knowing look with his pale lavender eyes.

"Right," said Joel. "Practising. Well, they'd better not be messing up my kitchen."

Ainsley frowned.

"And another thing," Joel went on. "Dad needs to stop handing Pippin over to the aunts. He needs to start actually spending some time with the kid. The boy's confused, and he's way behind on his speech. I'm worried about him."

"What about *me?*" Ainsley spluttered. "I'm thirteen years old and my life is already in the pits. Someone needs to worry about me for once!"

Joel rolled his eyes again and took another handful of popcorn. "Give me a break. Besides, you've got *Aunt Toppy*," he mimicked. "That old witch has got you covered."

"True," said Ainsley, chewing thoughtfully on a kernel. "But Toppy says I'm not appreciated enough by the rest of you."

Joel snorted.

"Anyway, I'm out of here," Ainsley went on. "Some of the kids from school are going to teepee Mr Garrick's house, and I figure it's about time I participated in an extracurricular activity."

"Oh, really?" said Joel with a shrewd smile. "And what would Aunt Toppy think about that?"

"She supports it."

Joel shook his head in disbelief, then took another handful of popcorn before Ainsley set off.

However, as Ainsley began to walk away, Joel caught sight of Maggie moving through the crowd and his heart skipped a beat. This was the first time he'd seen her since the party the night before, and he had to talk to her. She was trailing behind a trio of girls that Joel recognized from homeroom, and although she briefly glanced Joel's way, she didn't smile or wave like he'd hoped she would.

He felt an ache in his chest. And that could only mean one thing.

Damn. I really do *like her*, he thought, surprised at himself.

"Ainsley!" he called after his brother, hopping down from the railing and deserting his post.

Ainsley turned, then frowned at the sight of Joel abandoning the queue that was forming in front of the Haunted House.

Joel jogged up to his brother and shoved the ticket roll and money pouch into Ainsley's free hand. "Cover for me," he said quickly.

"What? No!" Ainsley cried. "I've got to go teepee."

"Please," said Joel, already jogging away. He snapped his fingers at Ainsley and then pointed to the Haunted House. "Just for two minutes. I owe you one, little bro. And I *appreciate* you," he added with a grin.

Joel heard Ainsley's colourfully worded response as he ran into the crowd in search of Maggie.

He caught up with her near the Shooting Fish in a Barrel game. Her friends were a few paces ahead of her while she lingered behind. She gave a start when she noticed Joel at her side. Her expression momentarily brightened, then quickly clouded over.

"Hi," Joel greeted her breathlessly.

"Hello," she replied in a cool tone.

"Hi," he said again.

Suddenly things were awkward.

Great, he thought. *Now what do I say?*

He cleared his throat. "Hi," he tried again.

"You said that already," she told Joel.

"And I meant it."

Maggie looked to the ground, kicking at a pile of sawdust with her foot. "Did you?" she asked, looking up again.

"Yes," the word tumbled out. "Yes, of course I meant it."

Maggie pressed her lips together as though trying not to smile.

Joel felt a rush of excitement. Things were okay between them—he could feel it. He still had a chance.

"Listen," he began. "I want you to know… about last night… I didn't… I don't…" He fumbled over his words, suddenly wishing he could kiss her and almost bursting into laughter at the thoughts that were forming inside his mind.

I want to kiss Maggie Ellmes!

And, even crazier, he wanted to *tell* her that.

"Maggie, I…" he tried again, raking his hand through his hair.

Then, abruptly, her expression changed and her eyes turned stony again. She was staring at his hand. Confused, he looked down at his hand, too. His gut clenched when he saw Lexi's name and number branded in black eyeliner on his palm.

"Um … it's not what it looks like," he stammered, unable to pry his eyes off the heart Lexi had drawn at the end of her name in the place where the dot over the 'i' should be.

Maggie forced a smile, but there was no warmth in it.

"You don't have to explain your relationship status to me, Joel," she said dispassionately.

"But I … um …"

"Whatever," Maggie interrupted. "But you'll still help me with my problem though, right?" Her pretty jade eyes narrowed coolly. "Because that's all I need from you."

For a long moment, Joel simply stared at her blankly. He'd been so busy feeling bad about what had happened at the party that he'd completely forgotten about the curse.

So, is she upset because she liked me and she thinks I'm seeing Lexi? he wondered. *Or is she just mad because she thinks I won't help her with the curse anymore?*

"I'm happy for you and Lexi," Maggie continued impassively. "You guys make a cute couple."

"Oh," he managed.

Silence.

"So?" she prompted, tapping her foot on the ground. "Are you going to help me or not?"

Joel swallowed. "Of course I'll help you. I said I would, didn't I?"

"Good. Then maybe we should talk." She glanced over her shoulder to where her friends were hovering some distance away, looking on curiously. "Later, though," she added, almost as if she were embarrassed to be seen talking to him.

"Later tonight?" Joel asked hopefully.

"Just text me when you figure something out."

Joel nodded his head numbly then watched as Maggie turned on her heel and strode after her friends.

TWELVE

The Storm Is Coming

MAGGIE AWOKE WITH a start as a rumble of thunder drummed through the night sky. She sat bolt upright in her dorm room bed, clutching the covers to her chest as she gasped for breath in the darkness. Slowly she detached herself from the harrowing nightmares of curses and doom that had been hounding her all night.

Outside, a storm raged. Rain pounded against the building, rattling the leaded glass window panes.

Maggie strained her eyes as she peered across the unlit bedroom. She could just about make out Isla's shape beneath her covers on the other side of the room.

"Isla?" she called in a stage whisper.

There was no response. At least one of them would be rested for Monday morning classes tomorrow.

With a heavy sigh, Maggie reached across to her nightstand and fumbled for her water glass. She took a sip, cooling her dry throat, then returned the glass and patted the table for her phone. She tapped the screen and checked for messages.

Nothing.

Typical Tomlins, she fumed. *Diagnose me with a curse and then leave me to my doom.*

The wind outside suddenly picked up and the oak branches beyond her window tapped viciously against the pane, making Maggie jump.

She shivered and hugged the covers tighter. *He was probably just too busy with Cheerleader Lexi all weekend to give my critical condition any thought.*

Her heart gave a tug and she swallowed a lump in her throat.

Forget Joel, she told herself, squeezing her hands into fists. *I hope he and Lexi live happily ever after blah, blah, blah, blah. I hate them both.*

The rain was pounding against the glass even louder now. She drew in a deep breath, afraid the window panes might actually crack. *I can get help from someone else,* she decided. *One of the other Tomlins brothers, maybe. God knows there's enough of them...*

Maggie dropped back down onto her pillow and stared up at the dark ceiling, wide awake and utterly miserable.

"Isla?" she whispered again, louder this time.

Still no response.

Maggie groaned.

Then a bolt of lightning flashed beyond the window, illuminating the room for a split second.

For the first time since she'd woken, Maggie caught a clear glimpse of Isla's bed. Her friend was lying motionless on her back with one arm draped towards the floor. Isla's face was tilted upwards, her lips were parted... and, hauntingly, her eyes were open.

The sight made Maggie's stomach flip.

"Isla?" she gasped just as a rolling clap of thunder shuddered outside.

Maggie froze.

"Isla?" she tried again, a little louder now.

When there was no response, Maggie crawled out of bed and tiptoed across the room. She approached Isla's bed and peered down into her roommate's open eyes, but she was met with no recognition or reaction.

Maggie's heart leapt into her throat. She nudged Isla's shoulder gently with a few fingertips, but there was still no response. Maggie tried again, shaking her friend fully by the shoulder now, but nothing happened; Isla just continued to lie there, her eyes wide awake but otherwise totally unconscious.

With her pulse racing, Maggie hurried back to her own bed and retrieved her phone from the nightstand. She scrolled through her contacts list until she found Joyless's name, then pressed the call button.

A groggy voice answered after four rings.

"Ms Joy," Maggie choked into the phone. "Something's wrong!"

"Who is this?" Joyless slurred. "It's three o'clock in the morning."

"This is Maggie Ellmes, in room two-oh-six. There's something wrong with Isla!"

Suddenly Ms Joy's voice became more coherent. "What happened?"

"I-I don't know," Maggie stammered. "But I can't wake her. And she looks different."

"Different how?" Ms Joy pressed, sounding suddenly breathless. There was a series of fumbling noises on the other end of the line, as though Ms Joy were running.

"I-I don't know," Maggie stuttered again. "She looks..." She glanced at Isla. "I don't know... possessed or something."

Possessed.

Maggie turned the word over in her mind. She hadn't meant to say it—it had just slipped out. But now that it had been said, it couldn't be unheard.

JOEL SAT ON his bedroom balcony, his legs draped through the rusted railing as he watched the dark storm clouds congest the night sky. Specks of rain misted his bare chest, but for the most part, the storm bowed away from him.

It was three a.m. and he'd long given up any hope of sleeping. How could he sleep?

He checked his phone absentmindedly, re-reading the messages he'd received from Maggie for what felt like the hundredth time.

Hello? Any chance you could help a girl out with a curse today?

FYI it's annoying when you ignore me!

Joyless is on my case again. Maybe she's the one who's cursed me? I wouldn't be surprised if she was a witch. No offense.

Joel's heart sank. Of course, these were all before his little *indiscretion* at Casey's party. These were all before he'd messed up, and the messages had stopped.

Regardless, none of this changed the fact that he had a job to do. He had to help her break this hex.

But. . . how could he help her when he didn't even know what he was up against? The spell was strong, that was for sure. It had physically thrown him from her when he'd so much as tried to look at it. He couldn't break a spell that strong; he wouldn't know where to begin. Even Maximus, with his years of experience, would tell him not to touch it. Sure, a small hex would be relatively straightforward to break—but this was no small hex. And without knowing what was behind it, he didn't have a hope in hell.

No, he thought. *There has to be an answer. If I can trace where the curse is sourced, then I can bind it. I can block it. I can. . .* He bit his lip. *I can do something.*

He stared at the rain water as it pooled on the balcony around him. The gale was rattling the corroded railings fiercely now. Ahead of him, the dark forest sprawled, and Joel looked upon it as though he were its master. The trees swayed in the storm and the wind howled as it ripped through the bare branches.

He looked at his phone again. *3:12 a.m.*

The thunder growled, and Joel understood its voice at once. It was a warning.

He shivered.

Something bad was about to happen.

THIRTEEN

What Ails You

MAGGIE WALKED TO homeroom in a daze. Joel was already in his usual seat by the door. When Maggie walked in, he looked up. He met her eyes for a second, conveying something that she couldn't quite decipher. All she knew was that he knew something.

She bypassed his desk and walked straight to an empty seat at the back of the classroom. Isla's usual chair was empty—not that Maggie had expected anything otherwise. She knew full well where Isla was. In the hospital. Unconscious. Unresponsive. *Un-Isla.*

Maggie felt a stab of loneliness as she sat loyally beside the empty desk, waiting in silence for Mr Fitzpatrick to arrive. Blonde Lauren and Hilary were in their seats, undoubtedly awaiting an explanation for Isla's absence. But Maggie avoided their gazes. What was she supposed to say to them? She didn't have the answers. What if Isla's condition was serious?

Maggie swallowed hard. *What if she dies?*

A horrible thought kept replaying in her mind: What if her curse had affected Isla somehow? After all, hadn't The Incredible Psycho Madam Emerald told her that the curse might spread?

It's my fault, she thought wretchedly. *My curse made Isla sick.*

Her stomach knotted. How was she supposed to get through the day without Isla?

All of a sudden, her text message alert beeped from inside her school bag, jolting her back to the classroom. She fished around the main compartment of her bag and retrieved her phone. One new message. From Joel.

Maggie looked across the room to the back of Joel's head. She opened the message.

What's wrong? Your aura is black today.

Quickly ensuring that Mr FitzP was still nowhere in sight, she typed out a response.

Isla is really sick. No one knows what's wrong with her, and it's all my fault. She furrowed her brow. *And your fault, too*, she added before pressing send.

A moment later, her phone beeped again.

How is it my fault?

You won't help un-curse me and now my curse has cursed Isla.

Don't be crazy, Joel responded.

This time Maggie didn't reply.

Her phone beeped again. It was Joel, again.

I'm sorry, was all it said.

Blinking back tears, Maggie let her phone fall into her bag. Then the classroom door swung open and Mr Fitzpatrick hurried in, looking even more flustered than usual. He dropped his briefcase on the edge of his desk and hastily knotted his tie.

"Morning," he grunted. His cheeks were ruddy from rushing and he was short of breath.

Joel cast a quick glance over his shoulder. He caught Maggie's gaze and held up his palms, as if wondering why she hadn't texted him back. She turned away.

Mr Fitzpatrick shuffled through his paperwork before eventually taking roll call. When he reached Isla's name, he skirted awkwardly around it, then read on.

"Where's Isla?" Blonde Lauren whispered now.

Maggie took a deep breath and turned to face her friends. "She's sick," she whispered back. "Really sick. It happened in the night."

Hilary's eyes widened, magnified behind her huge thick-rimmed glasses. "What's wrong with her?"

Maggie shrugged and looked down at her desk. She wished she knew.

"Are her parents coming?" Blonde Lauren whispered.

Maggie shrugged again. "Ms Joy called them last night, but they said they had a ski trip they couldn't postpone."

The girls fell silent again.

When the bell for first lesson rang out, Maggie gathered her school bag and plodded glumly across the room with the flow of people.

Joel was waiting for her in the hallway.

Maggie raised an eyebrow. "What?" she muttered. "Please tell me you've got good news."

"I have. I'm going to help you."

Maggie folded her arms. "You said that already."

"But now I'm communicating," Joel pointed out.

"I guess," Maggie replied dolefully. "It's a step in the right direction, I suppose."

Another classroom door opened and more students began to flood the hallway as they headed robotically to their morning classes.

"I promise," said Joel over the growing din. "This is going to be okay. I just need time."

Maggie nodded vaguely as Blonde Lauren and Hilary approached. She mustered a smile at them.

"See you, Joel," she said, turning her back on him to trail behind her friends as they made their way towards their first lesson.

"See you, Maggie," he replied to her retreating figure.

THAT AFTERNOON JOEL caught a ride home in Charlie's Mustang. The car was awash with Charlie's buoyant energy and drove how Charlie moved—erratically. Although the boys had been friends for some time, they had only started socialising outside of school in the last year or so, around the time Charlie had gotten his driver's licence. Sometimes Joel wondered if he was drawn to Charlie's energy or the car's—but either way, Joel was glad of the friendship. Charlie was, just like his car, alive with cavalier energy.

The Mustang swerved sharply into the wooded hills, following the narrow path that led up to the old mansion. Joel couldn't help but cringe as he saw Charlie's aura change to a murky blue when the dilapidated building appeared before them.

Fear, Joel noted with a sigh.

"Whoa," Charlie breathed. He hastily cleared his throat. "Is this your place?" He looked at Joel in the passenger seat. "I mean. . . man, it looks different in the daylight," he finished.

"Yep," Joel muttered, unfastening his seatbelt and climbing out of the car. He sighed again.

Charlie's grip tightened on the steering wheel. "It's cool, though," he added. "It's cool." All six-foot-four of Charlie's enormous build suddenly cowered in the presence of the imposing old building.

Joel decided not to invite his friend in. Despite his efforts in the kitchen, the rest of the house still wasn't ready for visitors. So he signalled a goodbye to Charlie and made for the front porch.

The family Jeep was nowhere in sight, suggesting that Evan and Maximus were probably out on some secret Chosen One business again.

Joel opened the rickety front door and was met with an unusual sight.

Ainsley was lying on his back in the front entryway, making snow angel shapes on the beat-up hardwood floor as he expelled ghostly moans of pain. Alleged Aunt Topaz's hunched elderly form was pacing around him, misting him with water from a spray bottle.

Joel's shoulders sagged. "What's wrong with you?"

Ainsley groaned. "Burning. Burning like fire."

Joel studied him dubiously. "You're sick?"

"I'm..." Ainsley's voice quavered. "I'm ill, Joel. The darkness has me."

Suddenly Joel thought of Isla and her mysterious condition that had Maggie so worried.

"What's wrong with you?" he pressed, nudging Ainsley with his foot.

"I have... P... M... T," Ainsley sobbed out the final *T*.

Joel pursed his lips. "You don't have PMT. That's a girl thing."

"You don't know," Ainsley bawled, huge bulbous tears spilling from his angelic lavender eyes. "I have it," he insisted again as he curled into the foetal position.

Alleged Aunt Topaz took up her spritzing with even more gusto. "There, there, child," she croaked, looking down her hooked nose at him. "Release the fire."

Joel turned his attention to Alleged Aunt Topaz. "Stop filling his head with this junk. He's got enough complexes as it is."

Ainsley rolled over to face Joel again. "Don't trivialise my feelings," he snivelled as he drew his knees up to his chest and locked his arms around them.

Joel ignored him. "He hasn't got PMT," he said to Topaz. "He doesn't even know what that is!"

"Poor Middle Tomlins," Ainsley choked sadly.

Joel snorted. "Hey, if anyone's the Poor Middle Tomlins around here, it's me," he said, jerking his thumb towards his chest. "Now get up off the floor, Ainsley. You haven't got PMT."

Ainsley defiantly rolled onto his stomach while Alleged Aunt Topaz continued to mist him, murmuring soothing sounds in his direction.

Joel's gaze moved away from them and landed on Pippin, who was cheerfully playing on the staircase.

Joel's breath caught in his throat. "Topaz!" he shouted, stepping over Ainsley and sprinting up the stairs to scoop Pippin up from the hazardous staircase just a few treads away from the missing third step. "You're supposed to be watching Pippin!" He glared at his alleged aunt as he clutched the toddler in his arms.

"I'm caring for Ainsley," Topaz rasped back. "Ainsley is my favourite." She spritzed him with water again.

"You people are insane!" Joel yelled. "*I'll* watch Pippin. We'll be in my room."

But Topaz was too busy with her spray bottle to take any notice.

Grumbling to himself, Joel carried Pippin upstairs to his room at the end of the hallway and set him down on the bedroom floor. "There," he said to his little brother. "You can't hurt yourself in here. Just stay away from the balcony. And no more playing on the stairs, okay?"

Pippin blinked up at him with doe eyes.

"Do you hear me, Pip?" Joel urged, crouching to ground level to meet the toddler's gaze. "If you play on the stairs, you're going to get hurt."

Pippin smiled, wispy blonde curls creeping over his forehead. "You're going to get hurt," he repeated Joel's words.

A shiver ran down Joel's spine.

"You're going to get hurt," Pippin echoed again, his voice clear and precise. It was the longest string of words the four-year-old had ever uttered.

Something resonated deep inside Joel, but he shook it off. Now wasn't the time to fret over a toddler's dark musings.

"Just play here for a while," Joel told him.

Then he stood up and crossed his room to retrieve his journal from under his bed. He flipped through the aged pages, searching for an unbinding spell that he might be able to use on Maggie.

"You're going to get hurt," said Pippin brightly as he amused himself on the floor of Joel's room.

FOURTEEN

Out Came the Silverware

BY FRIDAY JOEL was no farther along with helping Maggie than he had been at the start. As far as he knew, Isla had not awoken from her comatose state. Worse, Maggie had given up asking for his help—which meant that she had completely lost faith in him, his witchcraft, his morals, and his word. And he could hardly prove otherwise. Not until he found a spell that might help her, anyway. He'd have to find a spell that could identify the hex, or at least the root of it. If only she knew how diligently he was working to make that happen.

Tonight, however, he would have to pause his pursuit. It was Halloween, and there was no time for research. That was because tonight—much to Joel's dismay—the Tomlins family was hosting a dinner party.

For most people in town, Halloween was a time for partying, trick-or-treating, or dressing up in torn clothes and fake blood. For Joel and his family, though, Halloween marked the start of Erridox, a welcoming of a new dawn—and the time of year when witches would begin their recruiting. Over the coming week, a coven would choose a human to recruit, then set out to take them through what Joel understood to be a deep immersion in some pretty dark witchcraft. The Luna phase was in its third quarter, and by the time the moon was full, the coven would have secured their human-witch hybrid. The human had no choice in the matter, of course, as was the way of Erridox.

The Tomlins clan was one of the few witch families that refrained from recruiting. For starters, they already had enough alleged family members and hangers on to account for; they certainly didn't need any more. But mostly, Joel knew, it was because the Tomlinses had chosen to live like regular civilians—and recruiting a non-witch human into a coven without their consent was pretty brutal by even the laxest civilian standards.

And besides, in Joel's opinion, there was no good outcome to the Erridox ritual. Ideally, the human would embrace the opportunity to thrive amidst a host of witches absorbing any power that they were offered. In reality, however, most humans were understandably hostile to the recruitment process, which led to two common outcomes: either the human would die during the dark spell, or else they would remain trapped for the rest of their lives as little more than a slave in a coven of barbaric, uncivilised witches.

Nevertheless, the festivities of Erridox were there to be enjoyed. Witch families would travel from town to town, seeking their recruit and dining with their kind along the way.

Tonight, the region's dinner party would take place in Blackheath, and the Tomlins family was playing host.

"Finally," Maximus declared to his boys, his chest puffed out with pride. "At last we're hosting Erridox in a home we can be proud of."

Joel swapped a look with his brothers, all of whom were seated on ascending steps at the foot of the staircase. He watched as Evan surveyed the cobwebs and cracked floorboards with a dubious look on his face.

"I just hope they don't want to spend the night," said Evan worriedly, his blonde curls catching the light from the oil lamp suspended in the entrance hall.

"Or use the bathroom," Joel added.

"Bathroom," Pippin echoed from Joel's knee.

Ainsley grimaced.

The Tomlins boys had worked tirelessly—for a total of thirteen minutes—to prepare the dining room and shut the doors to the other rooms to keep the respective messes hidden from view.

But even Joel had to admit that the dining room did look spectacular. Its arched black wooden door opened out onto a polished wood floor that set off the darkly stained beams which ran from floor to ceiling. Down the centre ran a long mahogany dining table laid with thirty china plates and matching side bowls, not to mention glistening wine glasses and the late Really Old Aunt Pearl's finest silverware. Even the crystal chandelier had been cleaned and fitted with bright new bulbs.

While the boys had set the table, the alleged aunts had been busy preparing the Erridox feast. The aromas of meats and spices had been wafting from the kitchen for hours, and the squawk of the elderly women bickering continued to reverberate off the high ceilings in the hallway.

The sound of a car engine approaching came from outside. The brothers jumped up.

Maximus, dressed formally in a shirt and black robe, straightened his shoulders. "This is it," he said, beaming from ear to ear.

His boys lined up before him, trying their best to look presentable.

The doorbell chimed. Maximus's and Evan's cheeks flushed an identical shade of red. Joel crouched down to tame some of Pippin's wild blonde tresses.

"Welcome," said Maximus smoothly as he opened the door to the cold night.

Joel looked up to see an imposing middle-aged man standing on their dilapidated front porch, flanked by half a dozen motley looking teenaged boys varying in ages between eleven and sixteen.

"Maximus," said the man in a low voice. "Erridox greetings."

"Jefferson," replied Maximus, offering his hand to the towering man. "How nice to see you again. Welcome to Blackheath. I've heard you've moved locally?"

Jefferson pretended not to notice Maximus's outstretched hand. "Yes. Nice to see you also," he said without enthusiasm.

"Thank you for hosting me and my boys this evening," he added, though his voice suggested anything but gratitude.

Maximus stepped aside and the army of guests began to trickle into the hallway. Then all of a sudden Joel's mind went woolly and time felt as though it were slowing down, just as it had done at the party the previous week. He squeezed his eyes shut. When he opened them, time was moving in fast forward.

"Joel?" Evan's smooth voice instantly grounded him. "You okay?"

Joel blinked and time resumed to normal speed. He nodded at his brother, then watched the backs of the guests' heads as the procession followed Ainsley down the front hallway, filing sinuously through the house like snakes bleeding into the dining room.

Evan was following behind the last of the teenaged visitors now, speaking to them easily and politely. He seemed completely unperturbed by their less than friendly mannerisms. Joel, however, couldn't even bring himself to look up as the newcomers filed by. He simply stared at the wall beside him, one hand resting protectively on Pippin's shoulder.

Maximus had closed the front door and was trailing behind the convoy towards the dining room. He paused to introduce the man named Jefferson to his younger boys.

"This is my second son, Joel," said Maximus. "And this is my youngest, Pippin." He gestured towards Joel's legs, which Pippin was now cowering behind.

Jefferson's cold gaze landed on the child and bore into him. Joel bristled and lifted his younger brother up into his arms, breaking the stare.

Jefferson's eyes rose to meet Joel's for a split second. There was something about his expression that unsettled Joel. Something cold and detached. But before Joel could put his finger on it, Jefferson turned and disappeared into the dining room behind the convoy of young men.

"Joel," Maximus hissed, his face like thunder. "Why are you just standing around? You're in the presence of one of the most prestigious covens in the country. Get in there and make nice." He nodded sharply towards the dining room before feigning a joyful expression and venturing forward himself.

Joel placed Pippin on the floor and crouched down next to him. "Go to the aunts," he said quickly. "You'll eat your dinner in the kitchen, okay? And then they're to put you straight to bed."

Pippin's violet eyes widened sadly. He pointed a chubby finger at Joel.

"I know," said Joel gently. "I'm sorry, Pip, but I can't read you a story tonight. Dad needs me to meet the guests."

Pippin touched Joel's brow.

"I'll check on you later," Joel promised.

Then he withdrew a pen from his pocket and scrawled a note for the aunts on the back of Pippin's hand. *Dinner in kitchen, then straight to bed.*

"Now go to the aunts," Joel told him.

"The aunts," Pippin echoed.

"And show them this." Joel tapped the black ink on Pippin's hand.

"Show them this," Pippin said, sticking a thumb in his mouth as he toddled away.

With a heavy sigh, Joel ventured towards the dining room. When he stepped through the arched doorway, his stomach plummeted. Sitting in one of the tall dining chairs was none other than Kaden Fallows.

Joel's mind began to race as the realisation dawned on him.

Kaden was a witch.

ONLY ONE MORE coven arrived at the Tomlins family's dinner party that night: the Leominsters, a husband and wife with their three young daughters in tow. The Leominster girls, all under ten, twittered amongst themselves and shot furtive glances towards the teenaged boys while the adults held court with the dinner table conversations. And for the majority of the evening, Joel simply kept his head down and ate.

The alleged aunts brought in serving tray after serving tray piled high with their concoctions. Each time they passed through the arched entrance, they cooed and clucked in adoration at the Fallows and the Leominster families—probably to ensure they could become alleged members of one of *those* families in the future if things went belly up with the Tomlins clan.

Although Ainsley wasn't saying much, Joel noticed him disparagingly sizing up the Fallows boys and casting cantankerous looks at the Leominster girls. Evan, however, seemed to be totally in his element. He was looking upon everyone with intrigue, intently listening to the elders and their stories of witchcraft. Occasionally Maximus would bring Evan into the conversation, but he seemed relieved that his other two sons had decided to keep quiet.

When the topic of recruiting arose, the atmosphere around the table prickled. The air suddenly became charged and everyone took notice.

"We are seeking a boy," said the Leominster woman. "As you can see, we've been blessed with three girls"—she gestured towards the three blonde, pigtailed girls—"and my husband and I would like a son to carry on the Leominster name."

"That's understandable," said Maximus from his place at the head of the table, patting the corners of his mouth with his napkin. "I must say, my boys have been a blessing." As he spoke, he gazed fondly at Evan, who was seated on his right. "Fine, young witches that any father would be proud of."

Joel resisted the urge to roll his eyes.

"Hmm," said Mr Leominster, his eyes narrowing slightly as he watched Ainsley stuff an entire flax seed bun into his mouth at once. "A young one would be nice. Then I can raise him in the way I see fit."

"How old?" asked Jefferson Fallows in his deep, commanding voice.

"Nine," Leominster replied. "Ten at most. I haven't come across any I like yet, though."

Of course Joel knew that there was more to recruiting than plucking any old kid off the street. There were criteria that had to be considered. The recruit had to be susceptible to witchcraft, first of all, or else they'd never survive the recruiting spell. How often had Joel heard the alleged aunts gossiping about how, back in the day, witches had often mistakenly recruited humans who were incapable of the initial spell? And none of the humans in their stories had survived the ordeal. These days, though, the screening process was supposedly much tighter.

Still. . . thought Joel with a grimace. He couldn't understand why any witch would take the risk. Then again, he hadn't been raised in a family that supported recruitment in the first place. Generally, to the Tomlins family, the whole ritual was bizarre and inhumane. Which made Maximus's willingness to host the Erridox dinner this year all the more curious in Joel's eyes. What was he trying to prove?

"Ours is the reverse case," Jefferson was saying now from his seat opposite the head of the table. "As you can see, I have many sons, but as of yet no daughters."

Joel looked warily down the table to where the six Fallows boys were seated. Each boy was different in appearance, ranging from fair and ruddy to dark and tanned. Some were short and stocky, others were lanky and thin . . . And none of them bore any resemblance to Jefferson Fallows.

Then it hit him.

They aren't his biological children. They were all born human. Joel swallowed down the lump in his throat. *They're all recruits.*

Joel's mouth went dry as he looked down the table with renewed interest. Kaden bore himself with confidence and ease, that was true enough. But the other five Fallows boys had dead eyes, empty of the life that had undoubtedly once occupied them.

"I have six boys," Jefferson continued proudly. "One a year for six years. All are fine young men, but my oldest"—he cast an adoring glance over at Kaden—"is my greatest achievement. My most accomplished, by far. He was offered to me at a young age, you see."

Joel froze at the statement.

He looked to the head of the table, but only Ainsley returned a raised eyebrow. His father and Evan, on the other hand, didn't have any reaction to Jefferson's revelation. Both seemed too focused on ensuring that the dinner party went off without a hitch.

"We're both blessed with fine boys," was all Maximus said, before directed a glowing smile at Evan.

"Yes, that's so," Jefferson acknowledged Maximus's words with a cool nod. "But now I want a girl."

For the first time that evening, Kaden spoke up. "And we have found her."

Jefferson's lips moved into a sly smile. "*You* have found her, my boy," he praised. "And so close at hand. You've done well."

Joel felt his stomach flip. *Wait. They're recruiting in Blackheath?*

Something about the notion made the whole recruiting ritual all the more barbaric to Joel's mind. Blackheath was a small place, and chances were he'd know the family whose child was unwillingly abducted. Suddenly, it was all hitting too close to home.

Maximus must have been sharing his feelings, because the news was enough to make him visibly tense. He began to squeeze his fist around his silver dinner fork, opening and closing it like a hooked fish's gills straining to take in oxygen.

Finally, Maximus spoke. "Congratulations," he said stiffly.

"Congratulations," the others echoed around the table. Incredulously, Joel found himself saying it, too. He winced at the sound of his own voice.

Maximus cleared his throat. "May I ask, have you sought permission from the parents?"

It was becoming increasingly difficult, Joel knew, for witches to strike deals with recruits' parents without the authorities becoming involved.

Jefferson's smooth smile slithered across his lips. "That's the best part. The girl's parents are out of the picture at the moment, which is what makes it such a coup."

Joel's heart rate quickened.

No, he thought, suddenly feeling sick. *He can't mean . . .*

"Some covens have stopped recruiting altogether," Maximus was saying through pressed lips. "My family, for one—"

"Recruitment is the only way to ensure coven supremacy," Jefferson sneered coldly. "Surely you cannot question that? Although," he went on, "I have heard the rumours that one of your boy's is a Chosen One?"

Maximus began to give way to a proud smile. He opened his mouth to speak.

"However," Jefferson continued, "these days, having a Chosen One simply isn't enough."

Joel noticed the fork in his father's fist begin to tremor with the sheer force of the grip around it.

"Right," Maximus replied tightly. "Are you're sure you've found a human able for recruitment?"

Jefferson gave another enigmatic sneer. "Quite sure. Kaden has already found her."

Joel's heart began to race. *No. No, no, no . . .*

"Kaden's mark has been placed upon her," Jefferson elaborated sinuously. "It is done."

FIFTEEN

In The Dead of Night

JOEL LAY ON his bed staring up at the ceiling. Somewhere inside the house, a grandfather clock struck four a.m. He groaned and rolled over onto his stomach.

He'd hardly slept at all—he couldn't, not after the revelations of the dinner party that evening—and what little sleep he *had* stolen had been plagued by recurring dreams of Maggie. In his dreams, she was always surrounded by that bright gold light. Then Kaden would appear, and Joel would awake in a cold sweat.

So Kaden Fallows was a witch—or, more accurately, he was the Fallows coven's most promising human recruit. A dangerously unnatural creation of a human bestowed with witch's powers. And, worse still, he had marked someone for the Erridox ritual.

Someone who was more than likely Maggie.

Joel sighed. He reached over the edge of his bed and patted the floor until his hand grazed his phone. Lifting it to eye level, he stared blankly at the screen. The bright digital clock display stared back at him. It read 4:03 a.m.

With another sigh, Joel scrolled through his messages and re-read all the texts from Maggie. All the texts begging for his help.

He glanced at the clock feature again. It was 4:04 a.m. now.

Is it too late to text her? he wondered.

He wasn't particularly clued up on text etiquette, but he figured it probably was.

Abandoning the idea of sleep, Joel rose heavily to his feet and plodded across the room. He slunk noiselessly into the corridor and began to creep down the stairs.

The muted glow of light from one of the lower rooms was casting long shadows across the wood floor at the bottom of the staircase. Joel traced the light to the kitchen, where he found Quite Old Aunt Ruby chanting over the flame of a candle that was dwindling in a brass candlestick.

When he surfaced in the kitchen doorway, Quite Old Aunt Ruby ceased murmuring and turned to greet him.

"Hello, my angel," she said.

Of all the alleged aunts, Joel had decided long ago that Ruby was his favourite. She had a kindly face and long silver hair that framed her tiny amber eyes. In fact, everything about Quite Old Aunt Ruby was tiny, from her petite frame to her mouse-like voice. Another reason why Joel liked her, of course, was her general illusiveness. They only ever seemed to cross paths in the dead of night. In fact, Joel was beginning to wonder if she was nocturnal.

"Hey, Ruby," he replied, stepping out of the shadows cast by the flickering flame.

At once he noticed her dressing gown and fuzzy slippers, which suggested that she must have moved into the mansion at some point without his explicit knowledge. He briefly wondered how many other alleged aunts and uncles had taken up residence in the sprawling dwelling without his knowing, but he pushed the thought aside. He'd long ago come to terms with the fact that trying to keep tabs on the alleged relatives was about as productive as herding kittens.

Regardless, Ruby certainly was no bother. Actually, tonight, he was glad to see her. She always seemed to know when he needed to talk.

"Something troubling you, Joel?" she asked.

"You could say that," Joel muttered, staring at the dancing flame atop the candle.

A rat scuttled across the floor. Quite Old Aunt Ruby gave it a quick toothless smile, then returned her attention to her alleged nephew.

"I see," she said. "And is this problem too big for one person to shoulder himself?"

"Yes."

"Can you share it?"

"No."

Ruby held up her quite old hands. "Then I cannot help you."

Joel looked up from the candle and assessed her with his gaze. "If I tell you something, can I trust you to not tell my father?" he asked. "Or Evan," he added with a wince.

Quite Old Aunt Ruby said nothing, but her gaze remained impartial.

Joel took that as his cue to continue. "There's this girl. . ." he began.

"I shall raise the baby as my own," Ruby declared nobly.

Joel wrinkled his nose. "No! God, Ruby, not that. It's nothing like that."

"Blessed be," she said, breathing a sigh of relief. "I'm far too old to raise babies."

"You're not that old," Joel replied kindly. "You're only quite old. Anyway, it's nothing like that. It's"—he cleared his throat—"witch related."

"Ah," Ruby murmured, raising a silver eyebrow. "Do tell."

"There's this girl," Joel started again, flinching at the memory of the gold light that had locked around Maggie in his dream. "This *human* girl. And she's been. . ." he trailed off, then lowered his voice. "She's been marked for Erridox."

The candle's flame flickered anxiously.

Both of Ruby's thin silver brows flew upwards now. "I see," she murmured, her tone guarded.

"And I said I'd help her break the spell," Joel went on.

Ruby's frail hand went to her throat.

"Only I can't break it," Joel finished. "Can I?"

He looked up and warily met Ruby's ochre eyes.

"Don't help her," Ruby's thin voice crackled.

Joel groaned and dropped his head onto the kitchen counter, burying his face in his arms. He'd been afraid she was going to say that.

"But I have to," he told his alleged aunt, mumbling the words into the counter top. "I promised."

"You cannot make promises like that, Joel," she said. "Your promise, foremost, is to your brothers and sisters of the craft. You know that."

"You don't understand," Joel muttered, lifting his head just enough to peer at her over his forearms.

"What is it that I don't understand?" Ruby challenged gently. "Do you owe her something? Are you involved somehow?"

"No," Joel admitted.

"Then what is worth risking your own life for?" she pressed. "Because, Joel, that is what it could cost. If you intercept another witch's spell—an Erridox spell, no less!—then with your life you may very well pay. It is an unforgiveable crime"

"But I. . ." Joel began, then trailed off. This time he had no response.

"Again I ask you, what could be worth risking your life for?" Ruby pressed.

Joel cringed. She had a good point. What *was* he risking his life for?

And then it dawned on him.

"Maggie," he whispered.

SIXTEEN

Take the Fear

ON MONDAY MORNING, Maggie was dressed and ready for school in record time. It was officially November, and the temperature had dropped. She pulled on her navy school sweater and tied her hair into a ponytail as she hurried down the boarding house's spiral staircase. She passed through the main floor hallway just as the other girls were beginning to emerge from their dorm rooms, bleary-eyed and padding towards the shower rooms in their flannel pyjamas.

If only Joyless could see me now, Maggie mused. *Not just on time, but early!*

She glimpsed up at a stained-glass window that was catching the early morning sun's rays. She paused to admire the patterns it was throwing across the dark wood floor.

If only Isla *could see me now*, she amended silently.

A week had passed and Isla was still unconscious in the hospital's critical care wing. But Maggie had a feeling things were about to get better.

In no time, she was outside in the orchard. Dawn's light bathed the bare trees with a soft pink hue. The air was fresh and crisp, and the only sounds were those of birds and squirrels rustling amongst the fallen autumn leaves.

Ahead, the gothic-style school building looked forsaken. The Tomlins family's silver Jeep was parked on the asphalt next to a few of the teachers' cars.

Maggie's heart began to pound with the knowledge that Joel was there—and that he had come to see *her*. She pursed her lips, resenting that feeling. Joel wasn't hers, and he never would be. Nor should she want him to be—he was a Tomlins, after all.

This is business, she reminded herself. *Strictly business.*

She quickly checked her phone again. There were no new messages, but the one sent from Joel last night stared boldly back at her.

Meet me at school before homeroom, was all it said.

And here they were.

Maggie crossed through the stone entrance that led onto the school grounds. She spotted Joel at once, leaning against the annex wall. He waved as she approached, his violet eyes seeming almost translucent in the soft morning sunlight.

"Hi," he said.

"Hi," she replied, noticing a dimple in his check that she'd never paid attention to before. Her heart rate quickened again.

"How's Isla?" he asked, casting a glance to the boarding house.

"No change."

They fell silent for a moment.

"So, what's this about?" Maggie asked at last. "Why did you want to meet me here so early?"

Joel smiled a little. "I have an idea," he began. "Well, actually, I have a few ideas. Quite a few... various ideas, really..."

Maggie made circular motions with her hand to hurry him along. "So what are they? Tell me."

He cleared his throat. "The thing is, telling you how isn't really going to work. I'm going to have to *show* you. And by that I mean test my ideas out on you." He broke into a hopeful grin. "Are you up for some trial and error?"

Maggie shrugged. "Sure." Then she paused and raised an index finger. "Hold on a sec. By 'trial and error', do you mean..." Her voice hushed. "Are you talking about spells?"

Joel nodded.

"Oh, fabulous," Maggie drawled. "And am I going to get hexed from this 'trial and error' plan of yours?" she asked him.

"You're already hexed pretty bad," he reminded her. "I doubt I'll make it worse."

She exhaled sharply. "You're not exactly filling me with confidence here, Joel."

He flipped his palms skyward. "It's trial and error, remember? Trial and error isn't supposed to come with confidence."

Maggie frowned.

"Odds are you'll be fine," Joel added.

Maggie's frown deepened.

"Okay," she accepted grudgingly. "I mean, I guess if there's a chance it'll help Isla. And *me*, obviously. And if you don't have any better ideas. . ."

"That's the spirit!" Joel commended. He patted her on the head and began towards the Jeep.

"Where are you going?" Maggie called after him.

"Where do you think?" he called back.

Right. She shivered. *Spells. That means. . .*

"My place," Joel answered for her. "You know the drill."

Maggie hesitated. A cold morning wind stirred, whipping at her ponytail.

Jeep keys in hand, Joel turned and looked at her carefully. "Problem?" he asked.

Maggie looked between him and the school. "I don't know," she said. "It's just that. . ."

"What?" Joel urged from beside the Jeep's driver's side door. A note of anxiety coloured his tone.

"It's just that I've never been early to school before," Maggie finished. "It seems a shame to ditch before I've even gone inside."

"Oh." The tension was gone from Joel's voice now. "I've never been early, either."

They both looked towards the oppressive stone building.

"So, should we go inside?" Maggie suggested. "Just to dip a toe in or something?"

Joel pondered it for a moment, then shrugged. "Sure. Why not?" he conceded, walking towards her. "It seems a shame not to."

Together, they paced through the annex and flung open the double doors. The school hallway was quiet and unlit. Wisps of weak morning light poured in through the tiny, high windows and glistened off the bank of metal lockers that lined the wall.

Maggie placed one foot in the hallway, keeping her other foot securely in the outer annex. Joel followed her lead, then looked over at her.

"Is this good enough?" he asked.

"This'll do," Maggie confirmed. Her gaze travelled furtively down the dimly lit corridor rolling out before them. "We're officially in school early," she whispered. "I guess I can tick that off my bucket list now."

Joel's nose wrinkled. "Wow. Dream big," he teased. "Can we get out of here now?"

"Yes, and quickly, before anyone actually sees us."

Without another word, they retreated into the annex and paced swiftly out into the cool morning air.

They closed in on the Jeep and Joel jumped into the driver's seat. He turned on the engine as Maggie clambered into the passenger seat beside him.

This was the first time she'd actually been inside the Jeep. It smelled like Joel, she realised. It was an earthy, fiery scent that made her heart flutter a little. A length of twine with a brass coin attached to the end hung from the rear view mirror. Maggie touched the coin with her fingertips and her skin tingled.

"What's this?" she asked Joel.

He cast her a sideways glance as he reversed out of the parking spot. "It's a charm," he answered vaguely. "A protection thing."

"Oh," said Maggie, withdrawing her hand quickly and tucking it into her lap.

Joel laughed under his breath. "It's *protection*," he reiterated. "Don't be scared. It's good."

"I'm not scared," Maggie said a little too quickly.

She sat stiffly in the passenger seat as the Jeep pulled out onto the main road and left the school behind.

Despite her waves of trepidation, Maggie was sure of one thing: she was safe with Joel. Somehow, something deep inside told her that was true. That she was *protected* with him.

But as they sped away from the suburban town and headed into the hills, she couldn't ignore the knot that had formed in her stomach.

"There's something you need to know," Joel said, breaking the silence that had formed between them.

The tone of his voice set off alarm bells in Maggie's head. *It's about Isla*, she guessed, her mind racing ahead. *He's going to tell me that she's beyond saving.* Her stomach lurched.

"Tell me," she urged.

"It's about Kaden."

Maggie immediately felt herself relax. "Oh," she replied. "What about him?"

Joel glanced her way, one hand resting on the steering wheel. It was almost as if his pale eyes were looking through her, she realised. Almost as though he were seeing something she couldn't.

"Kaden's marked you," he said at last.

"Huh?" Maggie's brow creased. "What are you talking about?"

"Kaden," Joel repeated. "You know, that new guy in school? The one you were talking to at the party last weekend?" he elaborated, his tone taking on a note that Maggie didn't recognise.

"Yeah," Maggie said, confused. "What about him?"

"He's the one behind this. He has a spell on you."

Maggie's jaw dropped. "*What*? You've got to be kidding, right?"

"Of course I'm not kidding."

"Kaden?" she breathed. "Kaden Fallows is a... you-know-what?"

"A witch," Joel said the word for her. "And yeah, he is."

"What makes you so sure?" Maggie asked, hearing her own voice echoing strangely in her ears.

"Because I'm sure."

"But..." she trailed off. Dumbfounded, she stared into the forest beyond the Jeep's windows. "Why would he do that to me?"

Joel didn't respond.

His silence sent a chill down her spine. She turned to face him now. "Do you think he has a spell on Isla, too?"

Joel flipped his palm skyward before letting it fall back down onto the steering wheel. "It's possible, I guess," he told her. "Unlikely, though. Anyway, the spell he has on *you* is the one we should be focusing on."

"What kind of spell did he put on me?" Maggie pressed, gripping the edge of her seat. "Is it a curse?"

"Kind of," Joel answered without looking at her. "It's a mark."

"A mark?" she repeated uncertainly. "What does *that* mean?"

"It means he wants you," Joel elaborated tautly.

Maggie's head was growing fuzzy now, and her heart was beating faster with every word Joel said.

"Wants me for what?" she pushed.

"It's complicated."

"Joel!" Maggie squealed, throwing up her hands. "That's not a sufficient answer!"

"I'm sorry," he mumbled. "I don't know how to explain it."

"Try," she told him, exasperated.

His eyes remained fixed on the narrow forest road as they moved steadily upwards through the hills. "He wants you. . . to be in his coven," he clarified at last. "He's recruiting."

"He's recruiting me to be in his coven," Maggie repeated, hardly believing the words she was saying.

Joel nodded. "It's something some witch families do. Not mine," he clarified quickly, "but some."

"Like Kaden's, for one," Maggie supplied, staring at him in disbelief.

Joel nodded again. "They find a human that they like, and then they mark them, staking their claim. Then, by the next full moon. . ." he trailed off before meeting her gaze. "It's actually a compliment."

Maggie's eyes widened. "Oh, well then," she exclaimed. "If it's a compliment then I guess that makes it all okay!"

"I didn't say it was okay," Joel said calmly. "I just said that it's a compliment. He obviously sees something in you that he likes. . . something he thinks he can work with."

"Ew!" Maggie squirmed in her seat. "You're making it worse."

"You asked me to explain it," he defended himself.

They sat in silence for a while as the Jeep continued to wind its way through the climbing hills.

Maggie clasped her hands together to stop them from trembling. What could Kaden possibly want from her? she wondered grimly. What had he seen in her that made her a good candidate for his coven? She shuddered.

"So Kaden put some mark on me because he thinks I'm good raw material to work with," Maggie summed up after a while.

"Basically, yeah," Joel confirmed.

"And what is it, exactly, that he plans to do to me?" Maggie asked.

Joel sighed. "There's a ritual. It turns humans into. . . into something else."

Maggie exhaled in a rush of breath. "What kind of *something else*?"

"I don't know how to explain it," Joel said again. "A witch, of sorts. But a synthetic version."

"What, with . . . powers and stuff?"

"That's best case," Joel uttered darkly. "As far as I know, human recruits absorb powers. Usually from a witch who's on the way out, if you know what I mean. Dead," he clarified anyway. "But more often than not, it's the human who ends up dead."

Maggie's eyes went wide and she threw her head back against the headrest. "What?" she cried. "You're not serious, are you? This has to be a joke." She stared pointedly at Joel. "This is a wind-up, right?"

Joel shook his head. "It's not. But we'll fix it, I promise. I'll take the mark off you. I'll block him somehow."

She studied Joel's profile. She could tell he meant what he was saying, however crazy it might be.

"And then what?" she demanded. "Will he try again? Will he retaliate?"

Joel didn't say anything as he negotiated a particularly tight turn in the road. The gnarled branches of the trees scraped at the driver's side windows, almost as though they were trying to reach inside. The protective gold coin hanging from the rear view mirror began to swing wildly and Joel tightened his grip on the steering wheel.

"I don't know," he admitted at last. "I haven't got that far in the plan yet. Let's just work on breaking the spell he has on you, okay? Besides, if he retaliates, it'll be me he comes after, not you."

Maggie's stomach flipped. "What will he do to you?"

Joel shrugged. "I don't care."

"Don't say that!" she choked. "What will he do?"

Joel didn't reply.

Maggie swallowed. "I'm scared, Joel," she said quietly. "For me *and* for you."

"There's nothing to be afraid of," Joel assured her, his eyes still trained on the road. "Everything's under control."

Maggie turned to the window without responding. To her, things seemed anything *but* under control. She sighed heavily, wishing she could go back in time. Back to before she'd ever visited Madam Emerald's fortune telling tent and found out about this horrible curse.

"Why did Kaden have to come to Blackheath in the first place?" she muttered.

Joel glanced over and gave her a meaningful look. He didn't need to say the words; she already knew the answer.

Kaden had come here for her.

AFTER MAGGIE AND Joel had driven the rest of the way through the wooded hills in an uneasy silence, the Jeep finally reached the clearing in front of the Tomlins family's house. The drive, which had seemed to last an eternity for Maggie, was suddenly over too soon. She looked up at the towering mansion, watching wordlessly as the wind banged the building's crumbling shutters against its ancient stone walls.

Joel cut the engine and offered Maggie an encouraging grin.

She summoned a nervous smile back, and together they climbed out of the Jeep. Side by side, they paced towards the old mansion. Her heart rate quickened with each step.

Don't be a baby, she scolded herself. After all, she'd already been to the Tomlins mansion once before, and it had been fine. *A spider fest, but fine.*

Oddly, as they ascended the steps of the ramshackle front porch, Maggie was met with a sense of warmth. Despite its grim appearance, there was something welcoming about the old building. Perhaps it was Joel's company that gave her comfort, or perhaps the sprawling house wasn't as hostile as it first seemed. Whatever it was, right at that moment, she felt okay. And that was good enough.

Joel heaved on the front door and it swung open with a groan. Seeing the entrance hall for the first time in daylight, Maggie winced.

"After you," Joel said, ushering her inside with a broad sweep of his arm.

Sucking in a deep breath, she took a big step over the threshold to avoid a rotten floorboard.

Ms Joy's etiquette lessons ran through her mind. *It is always proper to give a host a compliment upon entering the house.*

"Um..." she managed.

Joel directed her gaze to the left, where an archway opened out into a kitchen space full of a hodgepodge of cupboards and stacks of ancient pots.

"I did that," he told her proudly. "It took me all morning once."

"Oh. Okay. It's... nice."

His satisfied smile twinkled in his violet eyes. "You think so? I did it."

Maggie nodded politely.

Joel began up the wide staircase, avoiding the broken third step. Maggie followed in his footsteps to the upper hallway, then trailed him down the long dark corridor to the sanctuary of his bedroom. Once inside, she felt herself relax a fraction. It was nice in there; nicer than she'd remembered, anyway. Joel had done what he could to make it pleasant, and it had worked. The wood floor was clean and the peeling wallpaper had been covered with notes and photos. And with the morning light streaming in through the glass French doors, it almost looked cosy.

Joel crossed the room and retrieved a leather-bound journal from his bedside. He sat down on the edge of the bed—which he'd hastily made this time, Maggie noticed—and began flipping through the worn pages.

"Is that a witch book?" Maggie asked.

Joel nodded, but didn't say anything. His attention was on the handwritten pages.

Maggie tentatively perched beside him on the edge of the bed and tried to resist the temptation to peer down at the journal. However, she did glimpse parts of a few handwritten subheadings.

Evan's Spell To Sense Danger...

My Spell To Restore Calm...

Notes on Herbs...

Maggie sat quietly until he stopped on a relevant page.

"Here we go," he muttered to himself, angling the journal for Maggie to see.

She turned her head towards the journal and read the heading: *Tomlins Binding Spell.* Her eyes travelled further down the page. *One must only interfere with a witch's spell in extreme circumstances. For instance: (1) risk of exposure; (2) unjustified danger; (3) warfare...*

Maggie swallowed hard. She'd known her situation was bad, but she hadn't known it was *that* bad.

"This is the spell I had in mind," said Joel, pointing to the page. He tapped his index finger twice on top of the messy handwriting. "I can do this," he decided. "I think."

"Great," Maggie said, then gave a nervous laugh. "I think."

Joel rose to his feet and began pacing around his room, gathering candles from the shelf beside the desk and placing them systematically on the floor. He routed through a dresser drawer and pulled out a box of matchsticks.

"You can light," he said, tossing the matchbox to Maggie.

She caught it and crouched over the first of the candles that Joel had placed on the floor. She drew a match across the box's striking surface and it fizzed and crackled to life. She bent to light the candle, feeling the flame's warmth creeping ever closer to her thumb and forefinger as she waited for the flame to take hold of the wick. Her palms began to feel clammy, though not entirely because of the heat.

She inhaled deeply. "This all feels so..."

Joel looked up from the page he was skimming. "Final?" he supplied.

Maggie shot him a questioning glance. "Strange, more like," she amended as she began working her way through the rest of the candles that Joel had carefully arranged in a zigzag pattern on the floor.

"If it's too weird for you, the spells and witchcraft and all that—"

"No," Maggie cut him off. "It's not that. I want to do this. I've just. . . never done anything like it before."

Joel closed the journal and placed it on his bed. "If it helps, you won't actually have to *do* anything," he said. "You might not even *see* anything. But if you do see anything. . ." He paused and cleared his throat uncomfortably.

"What?" Maggie prompted as she struck another match. "What might I see?"

"Well, it's possible that the spell might move through me. And if it does, then I might seem like I'm in. . ."

"In *what*?" Maggie pressed, lighting the final candle.

"In pain," he clarified. "But it won't last long. So don't be scared, okay?"

Maggie's mouth went dry. "Okay."

Joel smiled. "You never know," he teased. "You might get a kick out of it."

"What, seeing you in pain?" She raised an eyebrow. "I don't hate you *that* much."

He grinned. "I don't hate *you* that much, either."

Maggie returned the smile.

"Right," Joel said, clearing his throat again. "So, take a seat."

Maggie obliged, once again taking up her perch on the edge of the bed. She grabbed a pillow and hugged it to her chest, peeking over the top.

Joel stepped into the centre of the candle arrangement. The flames created long shadows across the floor and walls, caging him in. He began reciting from memory.

"*Blood of my brothers,*

A witch's call,

Blood of my fathers,

A witch's fall..."

Maggie glanced towards the balcony. The wind beyond the glass French doors was building, driving through the rusted railings and shaking the trees in the forest beyond. She shivered as Joel went on reciting in a faraway tone.

"*A spell cast in darkness,*

A spell bound in light,

Break the connection,

Brothers, hear my plight."

The balcony doors burst open, almost tearing from their ancient hinges. Maggie let out a cry and clutched the pillow tighter to her chest as Joel suddenly dropped to his knees, gasping for breath. The candle flames reared until they towered over his stooped form, their shadows wrapping around him like dozens of black cobras.

Maggie stared at the scene before her, frozen in fear, as Joel continued his chanting, his words escaping in a rasp now.

"*Unbind and unseal,*

Broken, it shall be,

Blood of my soul,

Set the marked free."

A gust of wind extinguished the candle flames just as Joel dropped face down onto the floor. The shadows slunk back, recoiling over his body until they had vanished completely. The last of the wind ruffled Maggie's hair as it retreated back outside.

Maggie's heart felt as though it were in her throat. She didn't dare move.

"Joel?" she managed in a tiny voice.

He lay on the floor, silent and motionless.

"Joel?" she tried again. The word sounded insubstantial as it escaped her lips.

He groaned in response. Weakened, he rolled onto his back, blinking up at the ceiling.

Maggie gingerly rose from the bed and, still clutching the pillow to her chest, approached Joel. She stared down at him for a long moment, not sure of what to say.

"Are you okay?" she managed at last, gently nudging him with the toe of her shoe.

"Mmm-hmm," he mumbled unconvincingly.

Maggie lay on the floor beside him and trained her eyes on the long crack that split down the centre of the high ceiling.

"That was amazing," she whispered. "I mean, really incredible."

He rested his hand on his heart. "Yeah," he murmured. "It feels like it worked." He smiled to himself.

A warmth spread through Maggie. "Incredible," she said in awe. "You are. . ." she trailed off, afraid of what she might reveal.

She wanted to tell him that *he* was incredible, and wonderful, and all those other words that encapsulated him at the moment. The overwhelming desire to tell him so rocked through her like the very gale that had torn through the trees just seconds earlier. "You really are a witch," she said instead.

Joel nodded his head.

"It must be wild," Maggie concluded. "Being a witch, I mean."

For a moment, Joel said nothing. When he finally replied, his tone was careful. "Sure," he said. "I don't know any different, though."

Maggie blushed. "No," she agreed. "I suppose not."

"We're a family of witches," he explained. "We always have been, and we always will be. That's just the way it is."

"Was your mum a witch, too?" she asked without thinking

"No," he answered bluntly.

Maggie winced. "Sorry, I—"

"No," Joel interrupted. "*I'm* sorry. I just don't like talking about her."

"Okay," Maggie said softly.

When he spoke again, his voice had lightened. "You know, I never thought there'd be a day that you and I would hang out again."

Maggie smiled shrewdly. "Are we hanging out? I thought this was strictly business."

Joel laughed. "It is."

Maggie laughed, too. She suddenly grew aware of how closely she was lying next to him on the floor. And how she wanted to be even closer.

"What's it like?" she asked quietly. "Being you, I mean."

He rolled his head to the side to look at her and offered her a lazy smile. "Most of the time, it's good."

"Oh, yeah?"

He was quiet for a moment. "I see things," he said after a while.

Maggie propped herself up on an elbow. "You mean, like visions?"

Joel licked his lips nervously. "No, not visions, exactly. More like colours. And feelings. Things that other people don't seem to notice." He paused, uncertain, then carried on. "Take you, for example. Right now you're..." Again he paused, allowing his gaze to wander over the length of her arm and up to the very top of her head. "You're a pale pink right now. It's... it's nice. It makes me feel..."

Maggie held her breath. "What?" she whispered.

"It makes me feel good," he finished.

She exhaled softly. "What does it mean?" she asked self-consciously, picking at a splinter in the floorboard. "Am I always pale pink?"

Joel laughed. "No," he said with a grin. "Definitely not. You change all the time, depending on your mood. You're always kind of shimmery, though, which is also nice. But this colour," he said, gesturing to the air around her, "is more gentle. And you're not always gentle, believe me," he added with a wry smile.

Maggie felt her cheeks grow hot. "So, what colour are you right now?"

He smiled as he looked down at his own hand. "Purple."

"And what does that mean?" Maggie prompted.

"Fear," he replied truthfully.

His answer took her by surprise. "You're afraid of Kaden?"

He shook his head. "No."

Maggie met his eyes and he held her gaze. She wanted to ask him what he was afraid of, but she couldn't find her voice.

"Now you're afraid, too," Joel murmured, his eyes still locked on hers. "Can I take it away?" he asked quietly.

Maggie blinked at him. "Take what away?" she said in a weak voice.

"The fear," he replied.

She managed a nod.

"You have to say it," Joel told her. "Invite me."

Maggie swallowed. "Take the fear away."

Joel drew in a long breath. Then, very slowly, he reached out and placed his hand against her cheek. She closed her eyes and leaned into his touch, relishing the comfort of his skin on hers. Her cheek began to tingle and her head grew fuzzy. As her eyes fluttered open, she was sure she saw a faint indigo glimmer trickling over Joel's arm, moving away from her and into him.

She felt calm all of a sudden. At peace. Her heart rate slowed and her body felt light.

"There," said Joel, finally dropping his hand.

In a dreamy state, Maggie reached up to touch the spot on her cheek where his hand had just been.

"What did you do?" she asked, sinking back down onto the cool floorboards and gazing up at the ceiling once more.

"I took it away," Joel said simply.

"Where did you put it?"

"It's here," he said. He looked down at something unseen in the palm of his hand, then made a fist as though he were squashing it. "How do you feel?" he asked, looking down at her with a nervous smile. "I've never done that to a human before."

"I feel..." she began, searching for words. "I feel calm."

"Good. You look it." He released a tense breath and laughed. "I mean, you look... pink."

She laughed, too. She gazed up at him, wishing he was closer. All she had to do was reach out to him, he was so near. But her eyes were heavy all of a sudden, and then she was falling asleep.

SEVENTEEN

Nothing To See Here

MAGGIE AWOKE TO the sound of a door banging somewhere inside the old mansion. She sat bolt upright, detaching herself from the deep sleep that had claimed her for the last who knew how many hours. She looked around Joel's room. It was dark beyond the balcony, and the drapes were stirring gently in the cold evening breeze.

Beside her, Joel sat up, too. He was wide awake now. Sober.

They both were.

Joel stood up swiftly, shaking off the sentimental expression he'd been wearing earlier.

"I . . . uh . . ." he stuttered. "I think I made us *too* calm."

Maggie rubbed her bleary eyes. "What time is it?"

Joel glanced to the moon, which was hanging high in the ebony sky. "I think it's safe to say that it's night time."

Maggie groaned. She took her cell phone out of her pocket and touched the screen. It flashed 12:06 a.m.

She groaned again. *Joyless will be on the warpath if I'm not back in my room soon*, she thought.

Joel paced to the bedroom door and peered out into the upstairs hallway. "Maximus?" he called out in a barbed voice.

There was no response.

"All clear," Joel said, poking his head back into the bedroom. "Come on, let's get you back to the dorm."

She followed him into the darkened hallway and down the stairs. Just when they'd cleared the broken third step, a frail voice reached them from the direction of the kitchen.

"Joel, my dear?"

Maggie watched as Joel frowned.

"It's my aunt, Ruby," he explained. "She only comes out at night."

"What, is she a vampire or something?" Maggie joked.

"I don't really know *what* she is," Joel replied offhandedly.

Maggie shuddered. "Well, the fear's back."

Joel shot her a quick grin. "Relax. Of all my extended family"—he used air quotes around the word family—"Aunt Ruby is the least offensive."

"How hard could it be to be less offensive than the Incredible Psycho Madam Emerald?" Maggie muttered.

Joel grabbed her arm and led her down the last two steps. "Come on. If we're lucky, maybe she didn't hear us—"

Suddenly, a tiny silver-haired lady was standing at the foot of the stairs, a wooden spoon clutched in one hand.

"Ruby," said Joel as he led Maggie the rest of the way down the stairs. "This is Maggie."

Ruby broke into a toothless grin. "Oh, I see!" She gave a rattily chuckle.

"Nice to meet you," said Maggie, trying not to grimace.

Ruby scuttled towards Maggie and gave her a quick hug.

Although Maggie was frozen like a startled rabbit, Joel seemed pleased by the interaction.

"She likes you," he whispered. Then he cleared his throat and raised his voice to address Ruby. "What are you making?" he asked, nodding at the spoon in her hand.

"Soup!" she replied quickly.

Joel rubbed his hands together. "Nice," he said. "What kind?"

The elderly woman shot a brief and surreptitious glance at Maggie. "Just your ordinary soup. Nothing to see here."

Maggie cast a glance into the kitchen and caught sight of a huge black pot boiling away on the stove. The ingredients piled up on the kitchen counter didn't look like any ordinary soup ingredients that Maggie had ever seen before. She tried not to retch at what looked like a pile of dead rats heaped up on the work surface.

The sound of a car engine arriving outside interrupted her thoughts.

The wooden spoon that Ruby was clutching in her tiny hand suddenly dropped to the hardwood floor with a clatter. "They're here," she rasped under her breath.

Joel visibly bristled as he glanced towards the front doorway. Male voices were drifting in from the mansion's front porch now—one of which Maggie recognised as belonging to Joel's older brother, Evan.

Then the heavy front door swung open and Evan was standing there beside by a middle-aged white-haired man whom Maggie took to be Maximus Tomlins, a man she'd never actually met before.

The newcomers greeted them, eyeing Maggie with curious intrigue. Evidently, they weren't used to strangers in their home—especially at this late hour.

Joel didn't reply to his father's greeting. "Who's looking after Pippin?" he asked instead, his tone clipped.

Evan looked awkward for a second, then busied himself closing the front door.

"Topaz is caring for Ainsley and Pippin," Maximus replied casually. "They'll be home soon, I'm sure."

Joel gave way to an angry breath. "They're not home? It's past midnight," he said testily. "Pippin's four years old, for god's sake. He needs a regular bedtime. He needs sleep—"

He cut his sentence short, as though abruptly remembering that Maggie was observing the entire exchange.

"Forget it," he muttered. Then, turning to Maggie, he said, "Come on, let's go." He took her arm and steered her towards the front door.

Maximus had already wandered into the kitchen with Quite Old Aunt Ruby, leaving the conversation behind. Evan remained standing steadfastly in front of the front door, his eyes glued to his brother.

"Where are you going?" he asked Joel.

"I'm taking Maggie home," Joel said distantly.

"Are you coming back?" Evan asked.

Joel led Maggie past Evan to the front door. "Of course," he muttered as he ushered her outside.

Then the sound of the door slamming behind them echoed through the bitter cold night.

MAGGIE FELT A strange mixture of relief and sadness when Joel pulled the Jeep into the school parking lot and cut the engine. Relief because he'd gotten rid of the curse, but sadness because that meant their time together was over. They'd go back to being acquaintances, and she'd watch from the sidelines as he and Lexi formed whatever whirlwind relationship was on the cards for them.

Joel eyed her now as she unbuckled her seatbelt.

"Is everything alright?" he asked.

Maggie blushed. "Why, what colour am I?"

He bit his lower lip, trying and failing to hide a smile. "Green."

She frowned. "What does that mean?"

He turned his attention to the steering wheel. "It means that you're... that something's bothering you," he answered vaguely.

Maggie drew in a deep breath. "Nope," she said. "I'm fine. Great, actually, seeing as I'm not cursed anymore. Thanks for that, by the way," she added lightly.

"No problem," said Joel as he unbuckled his seatbelt. "Come on, it's late. I'll walk you back to your dorm."

"You don't have to," said Maggie, gazing beyond the vehicle's windscreen to the high stone wall encircling the pathway that led to the boarding house.

"I want to," he told her.

Before she could protest again, he opened his door and stepped out into the deserted parking lot.

Maggie climbed out of the Jeep after him, and together they began towards the orchard that separated the school from the boarding house. Their footsteps fell in sync as they walked, crunching over the remnants of the autumn leaves.

Somewhere in the distance, an owl hooted.

"Thank you, Joel," said Maggie at last, her voice full of meaning this time. "You . . . you didn't have to."

Joel glanced at her wryly as they passed one particularly twisted apple tree. "Oh yes, I did," he disagreed. "Otherwise you'd never stop harassing me."

Maggie forced a smile. "Well, I can assure you that I won't be harassing you anymore."

Joel fell silent. "Okay," he replied after a while. "Good to know."

They neared the boarding house's huge oak door. As Maggie rummaged around in her shoulder bag for her key, Joel stuffed his hands into his jacket pockets, his gaze moving along the old building's grey stone walls.

"Home sweet home," he remarked.

"Yep. Home sweet home," she echoed, hearing a familiar sadness in her voice.

"I haven't been here in a while," Joel noted.

"Nope. I guess you haven't."

He grew wistful for a moment. "Remember when you first moved here, and we used to meet in the orchard at summertime?"

"Yeah," Maggie laughed softly. "We were just kids back then."

"Yeah," Joel agreed. He gave her a playful nudge. "It was fun, though, wasn't it? Playing in the grounds when no one else was around, building apple tree forts . . ."

Maggie laughed openly now. "Yeah, and hiding from Joyless!" She pursed her lips. "I guess things haven't changed *that* much."

"What's it like these days?" Joel asked thoughtfully. "Living here, I mean."

She shrugged. "It's okay. It was a whole lot better when Isla was here, though. Now my room feels lonely. And tainted."

Joel glanced to the front door, then back to Maggie. "Can I see it?"

She frowned. "What, my room?"

"Yeah," Joel said with a cautious smile. "You've seen my room, so it's only fair. Right?"

Maggie held her door key in her palm. "You do realise Joyless is the night manager? If she catches you trying to sneak in, she'll kill you."

Now it was Joel's turn to shrug. "I'll take my chances," he said with a wink. "Besides, I'm much better at hiding than I used to be."

Maggie twisted the key in the lock. "Don't say I didn't warn you," she whispered as the door groaned open.

They crept into the dark entry hall and were met by the homey scent of candle smoke and wood. Only one light was on, and it was leaking from the hatch window of Ms Joy's office.

Maggie's eyes widened and she looked at Joel. "Joyless is still awake," she mouthed, thumbing towards the office.

He inhaled deeply and then began muttering a string of words.

"*Clear as day,*

Your eyes will see,

All that is before you,

But you won't see me."

Then, without even a pause, he carried on walking towards the main staircase, directly passing Ms Joy's office.

"No!" Maggie hissed, waving her arms frantically in an attempt to catch his attention. But Joel kept on going, head down, footsteps light.

Maggie hurried after him. As she passed the office, Joyless looked up sharply.

"Maggie," she barked. "Just what do you think you're doing?"

Freezing on the spot, Maggie stared wide-eyed at Ms Joy. Joel was just a stone's throw away from Maggie's side, standing perfectly still as he watched the exchange.

"I-I. . . uh. . ." Maggie stammered. "I can explain."

"It's long past your curfew. Where have you been?" Ms Joy's pointed face craned out the office hatch window. As usual, her greying hair was pulled tightly into a bun and her wire-rimmed glasses were balanced on the very tip of her long nose. "Well?"

Maggie held her breath. Surely Joyless must have noticed the fact that Joel Tomlins was standing just a few paces away in the boarding house foyer. But why hadn't she mentioned it?

Did he manage to hide? Maggie wondered. She didn't dare look.

"I-I'm sorry," she fumbled for words. "I lost track of time."

Ms Joy made a low tutting sound. "Mr Fitzpatrick has already notified me of your unauthorized absence from school today. I suggest you get to your room at once," she snapped, gesturing towards the spiral staircase. "We'll discuss this in the morning. And perhaps after school as well—in detention." With that, she slammed her hatch window shut.

Maggie let out her breath and turned on her heel. As she hurried towards the staircase, she bypassed Joel, who stood grinning in the open. He followed her up the three floors of stairs and trailed her down the hallway towards her dorm room.

"How did you do that?" she hissed as they approached the door to room two-oh-six.

"I'm a witch," he replied simply.

Maggie quickly unlocked her room and they slipped inside. When the door clicked shut behind them, Maggie flipped on the light switch. She noticed Joel's gaze move curiously across the room, over the two neatly made beds and the combined collection of all of her and Isla's possessions.

Maggie felt a pang of sorrow as her eyes passed over the dorm room. It was half Isla's, too—but now Isla's side of the room was vacant and cold, with long shadows cast across the abandoned bed.

"She'll be back," Maggie said, half to herself. "If it's possible that my curse was what made Isla sick, then me being un-cursed will make her better, right?"

Joel scratched his head.

Maggie cross the room to the window and peered out at the waning moon high above the tree tops. Stars were scattered around it, shining down on her like kind, watchful eyes. Maggie unhooked the latch on the window and opened it onto the night.

"I hope she comes back soon," she said distantly.

When Joel didn't respond, she turned to look at him. His face was ashen.

"What?" she asked, her shoulders sagging. "You don't think Isla's going to get better?"

Joel shook his head. "It's not that," he said hoarsely. "It's you." His eyes flickered over her. "The gold light—it's still on you. I can see it."

Maggie's breath caught in her throat.

"Stand still," Joel instructed without missing a beat. He stepped up behind her and placed his hand between her shoulder blades. Then he recited from memory the first spell he had ever performed on her.

"*Granted sight,*
We seek in light,
Reveal, and see,
Show secrets unto me."

For a bated moment, Maggie was sure nothing had happened—apart from a slight tingling sensation on her skin where Joel was touching her, that is. But then, out of nowhere, Joel was thrown backwards across the room, causing him to collide heavily into the oak wardrobe on the far wall.

Maggie cried out, whirling around in time to see him slump to the floor. She rushed towards him as he sat upright.

"Damn!" he swore, pounding his fist on the carpet. He didn't need to tell her what he was thinking; she already knew.

"It didn't work," Maggie whispered, crouching before him. "I'm still marked."

AFTER LEAVING MAGGIE in her dorm room, Joel had sped home faster than he'd ever driven before. Why hadn't the spell worked? Was it because Kaden was too powerful? After all, Jefferson had described him as the Fallows coven's most accomplished recruit. If that was the case, then Joel would just have to work harder. He'd have to get better. He'd need to use more advanced spells. *Darker* spells, if that's what it took. His journal wasn't enough anymore, that much was clear.

He needed Maximus's spells.

So, as soon as he'd arrived back at his house, he'd crept through the sprawling mansion and stolen Maximus's journal from its hiding place behind the portrait of Really Old Aunt Pearl, all while his father had slept soundly in his bed.

Back in his own bedroom now, Joel moved in a daze. His head was fuzzy as he frantically flipped through the pages of his father's journal, getting drunk off the powerful spells he was practising alone in his room. But even as he lay drained on the hardwood floor, his head spinning out of control, he whispered one verse over and over again.

"*Darkest night,*
Hear my call,
A witch's blood,
The drops shall fall.
Bind thy enemy,
He cannot run,
Hear these words,
It shall be done."

EIGHTEEN

Worth Fighting For

MAGGIE AWOKE TO the shrill sound of her alarm. She sat up in bed with a jolt, her heart pounding. Her sleep had been a restless one, and it took several long seconds before the lingering unease from her nightmares began to slip slowly from her mind, replaced by the bright light of a new day. For once, she didn't hit the snooze button; her subconscious wasn't a place she wanted to return to at the moment.

As her eyes adjusted to the daylight that was seeping through the bedroom drapes, Maggie fumbled for her phone and checked for messages.

Nothing.

What did that mean? Had Joel given up? She winced at the thought.

If Joel's out of ideas, then I'll just have to figure out a new plan on my own, she decided. *A* better *plan.*

She certainly wasn't about to let Kaden turn her into a . . . a *something else*, as Joel had termed it. And if there was nothing more that Joel Tomlins could do for her, then she'd simply have to help herself.

Yep, she thought, straightening her shoulders. *I'll come up with something.* She pursed her lips. *Eventually.*

Maggie got ready for school in a daze. She dragged a brush through her hair as she picked apart her reflection in the mirror. Dark shadows hung beneath her jade green eyes, and her mouth was set in a tight line.

There is *one possible way around this*, she realised suddenly.

She drew in a deep breath and exhaled slowly. Yes, there was one obvious solution that hadn't been suggested yet. How could she have overlooked it? Without wasting any more time, Maggie gathered her school books and hurried out of the dorm room, hoping to avoid Ms Joy and the morning talking-to she'd threatened. Fortunately, the upper corridor was quiet and Joyless was nowhere in sight. It was still early, Maggie knew, and no one else had surfaced from their rooms yet. Maggie descended the spiral staircase and paced out into the crisp November air.

The trees in the orchard swayed as she raced along the pathway that wound through them. Ahead, she noticed a few cars in the school parking lot. Small cliques of students were already gathered beneath the annex, chatting casually amongst themselves.

There was no sign of the Jeep, however. And no sign of Joel.

Maggie bypassed the other students and headed straight for homeroom. She'd wait for him there.

He'll be here soon, she thought.

She was sure of it. There was no way he would ditch school after what had gone down the night before. He wouldn't just abandon her. At least, she *hoped* he wouldn't. She knotted her fingers together on the desktop and waited.

As the minutes ticked by, people began to file into Mr Fitzpatrick's room. Blonde Lauren . . . then Hilary . . . then Charlie . . . But still no Joel.

Maggie glanced at the wall clock.

Where is he? she wondered.

How could he be late today of all days? She was about to reach for her phone to text him, when she heard the classroom door swing open.

Maggie sucked in her breath and looked up.

But it wasn't Joel.

Mr Fitzpatrick strode in looking windswept and tired as usual. The first bell sounded just as the door closed behind him, and Mr Fitzpatrick called order.

Maggie slumped back in her seat, defeated.

BY LUNCHTIME JOEL still hadn't shown up at school, and Maggie was beginning to worry. Not only worry for herself, but for Joel also. What if something had happened to him? Hadn't he said that if Kaden retaliated it would be on Joel's head?

Maggie's stomach tightened at the thought.

Preoccupied, she merged into the cafeteria lunch queue. Dragging her tray along the line, she stared into space while the lunch ladies heaped dollops of unidentified ground meat and potatoes onto her plate. Numbly, Maggie took her tray and joined Blonde Lauren and Hilary at their usual table.

"Hey," she greeted the girls dully as she sank into her seat.

They looked at her, then looked at each other and frowned.

Hilary's eyes narrowed behind her thick-framed glasses. "What's with you today?" she asked Maggie.

"Yeah," Blonde Lauren added. "You've been, like, extra spacey lately."

Maggie sighed and prodded her food with her fork. "I don't know. I'm worried about Isla. And about . . ." she trailed off, not bothering to finish her thought.

The last time she'd brought up the subject of spells and curses, her friends had acted like she was losing her mind.

"About what?" Blonde Lauren prompted, flipping her flaxen hair over her shoulder and leaning in to hear the juicy details.

"I don't know." Maggie sighed again. "Joel, I guess."

The girls swapped another perplexed look.

"Joel Tomlins?" Hilary clarified, raising an eyebrow. "What about him? Is this because of what I said about him liking you?"

"No, it's not that," Maggie mumbled.

Hilary held up her palm. "Wait, he's not still trying to convince you you're hexed, is he?" She stifled a laugh.

Maggie prodded her food a little harder. She couldn't get into this debate right now. They didn't know what she knew. They hadn't seen what she'd seen.

"Never mind," she said instead. "Forget I mentioned anything."

"Do you like him?" Blonde Lauren pried, her blue eyes widening in excitement. Before even giving Maggie a chance to answer, she turned to Hilary. "Do you think Maggie likes Joel Tomlins?"

Now there's a question, Maggie mused. Did she like Joel?

She sighed heavily. How could she not? With everything that had been going on over the past few weeks, things had shifted between them. She and Joel had shared something; she felt safe with him and connected to him. He was . . .

Joel, she thought sadly.

"You do, don't you?" Blonde Lauren squealed. "You like Tomlins!"

"Shh!" Maggie hissed, glancing over her shoulder into the crowded cafeteria. "Keep your voice down!"

"I will if you admit it," Blonde Lauren whispered with a wicked grin.

"Fine," said Maggie, letting her fork drop onto her tray with a clatter. "I like Joel. There, are you happy?"

Blonde Lauren nodded her head emphatically. Hilary was unmoved.

"But it doesn't matter anyway," Maggie went on, staring down at her untouched food. "I think he's dating Lexi."

Blonde Lauren frowned. "Cheerleader Lexi?"

Hilary's brow furrowed, too. "Devoid-of-soul-and-basic-morals Lexi?"

Maggie nodded. "Yes, that Lexi."

Blonde Lauren's expression relaxed. "Nuh-uh," she said, shaking her head. "I happen to know for a fact that Lexi is hooking up with Sleazy Dale. They're a thing now."

Maggie's eyebrows shot up. "Lexi and Sleazy Dale?" she echoed. "How do you know that?"

"*Everybody* knows that!" Blonde Lauren cried. "And if you hadn't been such a space-case lately, you'd know it, too."

Hilary nodded in confirmation. "Even *I* knew about Cheer-tart Lexi and Sleazy Dale."

Maggie anxiously linked and unlinked her fingers. "But I saw Lexi and Joel kiss at Casey's party the other week," she muttered quietly.

"Yeah," Blonde Lauren replied. "Apparently she tried to kiss him but he wasn't interested. And then at the carnival he told her he was into someone else." Her eyes lit up again. "Hey, maybe he meant *you!*"

For the first time that day, Maggie smiled.

"Look!" Blonde Lauren shrieked suddenly. "There he is!"

Maggie turned so quickly that she almost knocked her tray to the floor.

Finally! she thought. *It's about time . . .*

But her bubble soon burst when she realised that it wasn't Joel whom Blonde Lauren had sighted.

It was Kaden.

Maggie tensed. Kaden was sauntering into the cafeteria, his dark hair styled perfectly around his strikingly handsome face. He had presence, Maggie had to admit. Charm. Charisma. Mystery. He was the sort of guy any girl would dream of.

But his darkness was frightening, and somehow Maggie was the only one who saw that.

She looked away, her skin crawling with the knowledge that he already had a hold on her. Distantly, in her foggy mind, she heard Blonde Lauren chatter on about how wonderful Kaden was.

"Would it be unethical of me to make a move on him while Isla is currently unavailable?" she was musing.

Hilary groaned. "Oh my god, Lauren. How could you even say that?"

"I didn't *say* anything. I just *asked* it," she defended herself.

Maggie dared to glimpse Kaden's way again, just for a second. However, a second was long enough for him to meet her eyes. His cool grey stare pierced through her in the most intrusive way.

Her breath caught in her throat.

Joel, she willed silently. *Where are you?*

JOEL LAY UNMOVING on his bedroom floor. He was awake—sort of—but he couldn't move. His eyes stared fixedly on the floorboards. He couldn't say exactly how long he'd been there like this; all he knew was that by the time he'd regained consciousness, it had already been dark. And now darkness had turned to light, and he still couldn't move.

His eyelids lowered. He'd heard about witches who'd died in this state; they'd gotten greedy with their spells, and their bodies had no longer been able to host the power. Was he destined to join their ranks? Was he going to die?

His eyes began to close.

No, he urged himself. *Don't give up. Maggie needs you.* He gritted his teeth. *Pippin needs you.*

Joel blinked, forcing himself to stay awake. His mind wandered back to a time four years ago—a time that had not only categorically changed his life forever, but had also *given* him a life worth fighting for.

He had been thirteen years of age, sitting at the breakfast table in their old split-level downtown and ignoring a bowl of cereal as he'd stared into space.

"Eat something, Joel," Evan had said to him.

Joel had blinked across the table at his brother. Evan had only been fourteen at the time, but somehow, even back then, he'd seemed so much older.

"I can't," Joel had murmured, looking down at his cereal which had long ago turned into a pool of mush.

"Please," Evan had begged, his violet eyes glassy. "Please, Joel, it's been days. You have to eat."

Joel had taken in a slow breath, wishing he had a response. But he hadn't been able to think of anything to say. He'd been empty, no more than just a shell.

"I have to walk Ainsley to school," Evan had said quietly. "Will you. . . will you be okay while I'm out?"

Joel had continued to stare blankly at the peeling paint, not saying anything.

What does okay mean, anyway? he'd wondered as Evan had left the house with Ainsley and closed the door behind them.

Had he been okay when his fish had died—when he'd taken the fish food to the tank only to find Flipper floating on the water's surface? Had he been okay when his mother had disappeared the first time, leaving a hole in his heart that had torn away at him every single second of every single day? Had he been okay when she'd returned, only to disappear again a few years later?

Am I okay now that Dad's gone, too?

Maximus had abandoned them with no warning four days before, leaving them alone to take care of each other with nothing more than a note to remember him by.

My boys, the note had said. *I'm sorry, but I have to go. I have to find her, and when I do, I'll bring her home and we can all be together again. We can finally be a family, just like we were supposed to be.*

Staring down at his mushy breakfast cereal, Joel's blood had boiled just thinking about that note.

Screw your idea of family, he'd thought vehemently.

And then he'd lifted his untouched cereal bowl and thrown it across the room. It had crashed into the tatty cabinets above the sink and smashed into smithereens. Thick, soggy globs of cereal mush had dripped down the cupboard doors and landed in a slopping mess on the kitchen counter.

Somewhere in the other end of the modest house, his newborn brother had begun to cry. It was a sound that Joel had spent the last few days ignoring. The mere idea of another baby had still been too raw in Joel's mind to process, let alone accept.

The baby's wails had grown louder—too loud to be overlooked any longer. And Evan wouldn't be back for nearly an hour.

Warily, Joel had risen to his feet and walked into the dim corridor, his feet moving slowly across the threadbare carpet until he'd reached the door where the cries had been coming from.

Carefully, Joel had twisted the doorknob and ventured into the room for the first time since the baby had arrived. The space had been full of unfamiliar things: a crib, a blue crocheted blanket, and a tiny squealing baby with tears streaming down its crinkled little face.

"Hello," Joel had said, peering down at the strange red-faced creature before him. "You know this is all your fault, right?"

The baby's wails had grown even louder, making Joel frown.

"It's true," he'd insisted. "If you hadn't shown up... Hell, if you'd never even been born, then Dad would still be here. And everything would be a lot quieter," he'd added, plugging his fingers into his ears.

But he had still been able to hear the crying.

"What do you want from me?" he'd asked the baby, dropping his hands to his sides once again. "Evan fed you already, and he changed you, too. So what's your deal, loudmouth?"

The baby had kept on crying.

"Shut up, already," Joel had groaned. "I can't wait until we can dump you on one of the alleged aunts. You're not part of this family. You don't belong here."

The baby's face had turned tomato red and its cries were growing hoarse, penetrating Joel's every fibre.

"Okay, okay!" Joel had yelled. "Just shut up already!"

Then he'd lifted the tiny baby from the crib and held him against his chest. Against his heart.

"Is this what you want?" Joel had demanded. "You want a hug, loudmouth?"

The baby's cries had immediately eased, causing Joel's throat to grow tight.

"Oh, so you think being hugged makes everything all better?" he'd asked the baby; the anger had begun to leave his voice. "Is that what you think? Babies are so stupid," he'd commented, peering down at the child in his arms. "You're the stupidest baby I've ever come across."

Joel had begun to rock his baby brother back and forth in his arms, quietening him completely.

"I suppose you want to see around the house now, too," Joel had said with a sigh. "I can tell you're as nosy as you are loud."

He'd walked back into the hallway, cradling the cooing baby in his arms.

"That's mine and Evan's room," Joel had told his new baby brother, nodding towards a closed door at the end of the narrow hallway. "You're not allowed to go in there."

Then he'd turned and nodded at another doorway.

"That's the bathroom," he'd pointed out, then angled the baby in his arms. "And that's Ainsley's room. And," he'd said, turning back the way they'd come, "this is your room, obviously. It *used* to be Dad's room, but then you showed up and..."

Joel's voice had gone slack in his throat. How was he supposed to explain it when he hadn't even been able to make sense of it himself?

"Well, I think you're old enough to hear the truth," he'd told the baby frankly. "Dad's not coming back this time. He's abandoned us." He'd looked down at the baby again, his gaze softening. "But I suppose you know all about that, huh? They ditched you real fast. At least I had a couple of good years with them."

The baby had smiled at that, making Joel laugh.

"Babies," he'd muttered under his breath. "So stupid."

Then he'd carried on walking, back towards the kitchen and living room.

"So, this is where we eat and watch TV," he'd pointed out. "And that's the doorstep where you were left. And... that's pretty much it."

The baby had reached out a chubby pink hand and touched Joel's cheek.

Joel had cleared his throat. "I've decided that I *might* let you stay with us for a little while," he'd revealed. "The alleged aunts aren't very nice, and I guess you've had a pretty tough week—what with all the abandonment."

Joel had gazed around the room then, taking in the old sofa, the coffee table piled high with mail, the empty spot on the entertainment centre where Flipper's tank had once been.

With the baby still safely in his arms, Joel had sunk onto the sofa. He peered down at the remnants of a discarded apple core and his nose crinkled.

"Gross," he'd muttered, reaching down to retrieve the rotting core with one hand while still cradling the baby in the other arm. The core broke in half at his touch, spilling its tiny brown pips down between the sofa cushions.

Joel had groaned. The baby had cooed.

Looking down at the smiling baby, Joel couldn't help but smile back. "You're just a little pip, aren't you?" he'd said. "I'm going to call you Pip. Sir Pippin, the Prince of Tomlinsland. Do you like it?"

The baby had kept smiling.

Joel had smiled back.

"Yeah, I thought you would."

A voice interrupted Joel's memory, drifting into his mind as though projected across the astral planes. It jolted him back to the present with a bitter thud. Suddenly Joel found himself back on the floor of his bedroom in the ramshackle old mansion, where he'd been lying immobile for what felt like hours. Days, maybe.

"I'm coming for you, Joel Tomlins," said the voice, which was clearly meant to be heard by his ears only. "You wanted a war, and now you've got one."

Joel recognised the voice at once.

"Kaden," was all he could manage to say before he succumbed to the blackness once again.

NINETEEN

Complicated

JOEL AWOKE AGAIN to banging on the front door. He knew exactly who it was, too. And he had to get to her.

It took no small effort for him to get to his feet. Then, with speckled vision and unsteady legs, he staggered out of his room, into the hallway, and down the stairs. In his hazy state, he was unable to judge the broken floorboards with his usual precision, and loose nails and splinters cut into his feet. He almost broke his leg on the missing third step before stumbling to the front door and flinging it open, nearly tearing it off its hinges.

Through his bleary eyes he saw her.

Maggie. Surrounded by clear gold light.

Behind her, the wind rocked through the forest, and the trees cast dark shadows into the deep unknown.

Maggie's face, which had first appeared angry, melted into an expression of concern.

"What happened to you?" she whispered, her hands flying to her face. "You look like death."

"I feel worse," Joel muttered. He looked over her shoulder. "How did you. . . ?"

"I walked," she said simply. "I had to see you."

"Come in," he said, ushering her into the house and bolting the door behind them.

Once safely inside, Maggie placed her hand on Joel's arm. However, he soon recognised that she wasn't seeking comfort; rather, she was steadying him as he swayed.

"Joel," she breathed. "What's wrong with you?"

He raked his hand through his hair. "I've tried everything, Maggie," he half choked. "And I can't get him off you. I can't get rid of him." He spat out the final word through clenched teeth. The very thought of Kaden infesting her tore him up inside.

"I was worried," Maggie went on, her voice quiet and trembling. "When you didn't show up at school today, I thought something might have happened to you."

"His hold is too strong," Joel went on, as if she hadn't spoken at all. Not for the first time, he wondered how a human-born recruit had accumulated such vast powers as a witch; it made no sense. "I've tried everything, but it's still on you . . ."

He reached out and trailed his fingers along a strand of her honey coloured hair. There, in the cool evening light of the entrance hall, with the day's last rays of sun spilling through the tall windows, Joel could see the golden glow of the spell on Maggie. He saw it as clear as day, as if it were a physical part of her being. All of his spells and casting had done nothing to help her; all they'd done was leave him broken of body and hazy of mind.

Maggie inhaled and closed her eyes at his touch.

Scarcely thinking, he drew her into him and held her in his arms. He breathed in the sweet scent of her hair as they stood entwined in the hallway, their hearts beating quickly as one.

I can't let Kaden take her. His stomach lurched at the thought.

Why had it taken *this* for him to realise how he felt about her? She meant so much to him—enough to risk his life for. Why hadn't he recognised it before?

Maggie was the only girl that saw him for who he *really* was. She wasn't charmed by his witchcraft, or frightened of him, or awestruck by his uncommon looks. When she looked at him, what she saw was just *him*—and he saw her too, warts and all.

Even from the very first day he'd met her, he'd known that she was something special. She'd been a feisty pre-teen when she'd first shown up in Blackheath, the resident new girl in school and the newest addition to the old boarding house, where she'd had to live because her family couldn't care for her.

Abandoned, Joel had thought at the time.

It had been something he could empathise with, seeing as he'd already been left by his mother once.

They'd been friends, sure. But then they'd grown up, and things had gotten. . .

Complicated, Joel thought now.

But it wasn't complicated anymore. Now it was just him and her. And there was no way he was going to let Kaden take her. He wasn't going to lose her all over again.

"Will it hurt?" Maggie whispered into his chest. "When they make me a witch, I mean."

He pulled away and met her eyes. It broke his heart to see the faint glimmer of purple shining through the gold.

"It won't happen," he said firmly. "I told you, I won't let it. I'll find a way."

She buried her face in his chest again, and he nestled his chin on top of her head. They stood that way, fused together, listening to the wind as it rattled the window panes.

"It's going to be okay," Joel promised her.

But even as he said the words, the voice from earlier was still speaking to him. It was taunting him at a level heard only by his own ears.

"I'm coming for you," Kaden hissed.

TWENTY

The Full Moon

AS THE SUN began to set, Maggie went out and stood on Joel's bedroom balcony to watch the iridescent blues and purples of twilight darken the forest. It was quite beautiful, really. She found herself wondering if she would still be able to appreciate this if she was turned into a witch. Would she still have her own thoughts and feelings?

She gazed at the faint outline of the full moon that was just beginning to show itself, in the limbo of night and day.

Like it or not, she was still marked. And Kaden was coming for her.

She glanced over her shoulder at Joel, who was working tirelessly in the room behind her. He was scattering herbs on a candle flame and muttering words that she couldn't quite decipher. He was trying so hard—and he was doing it all for her.

He was broken, barely able to walk or speak, and yet he kept trying. She could almost feel his pain as though it were surging through her own veins. She knew that very soon, for his sake, she would beg him to stop.

Her thoughts were interrupted when her phone began to ring from inside her jacket pocket. She withdrew it warily, unsure of who might be calling her. Probably Ms Joy, wondering why she'd skipped afternoon classes and missed detention to boot.

Maggie glanced down at her phone and saw Isla's name flash across the screen. Her heart skipped a beat. She hurriedly pressed answer and held the phone to her ear.

"Isla?" she exclaimed. Her voice was dwarfed by the wind that was whipping at her hair as she held onto the balcony railings.

"Mags," Isla's voice returned to her, weak but there.

Maggie's eyes brimmed with tears at the sound of her friend's voice. "You're awake!" she exclaimed.

"Yeah," Isla replied with a soft giggle. "I'm awake. Ms Joy said I'd been out for a while."

"I can't believe I'm actually speaking to you." Maggie laughed in a rush of emotion. "It's been so long."

"Really?" came Isla's reply. "Weird. I feel like I just spoke to you yesterday!"

"What did the doctors say?"

Isla gave an audible yawn. "They think I picked up a virus or something," she explained. "They want me to stay in the hospital tonight, just to make sure it's passed. But I should be able to come back to the dorm tomorrow."

Maggie exhaled in relief. "That's great news, Isla."

"Where are you?" Isla asked.

"I'm at Joel's house." She glanced over her shoulder again and caught sight of Joel. He was reading intently from his journal, his lips moving silently. "And I think I'm going to be here for a while," she told her friend.

"Joel Tomlins?" A note of surprise coloured Isla's voice. "Whoa. How much have I missed?"

"We've. . ." Maggie trailed off, searching for words. "We've kind of been hanging out, I guess."

"You and Tomlins, huh?" said Isla. "Whatever floats your boat. Besides, that leaves more Kaden Fallows for the rest of us," she added with a mischievous titter.

Maggie swallowed, unsure of what to say. How was she supposed to explain all this?

Hey Isla, glad you've woken up from your coma. And oh, by the way, the guy you like is a witch and he's trying to recruit me into his coven.

"Well, I think you should go for it with Joel," Isla's voice interrupted her thoughts. "I've always figured you two were soulmates." She gave a sleepy laugh.

Maggie snorted. "Since when?"

"Since always!"

"You've never said that before."

Isla sighed impatiently into the phone line. "That's because you always insist you hate each other. When really everybody knows you've loved each other since you were kids." She erupted into giggles.

Maggie felt herself blush from ear to ear. She could hardly believe she was having this conversation on Joel's balcony, with

Joel in the room behind her. Not to mention the fact that it seemed way too light-hearted and normal as compared to how everything else had been going lately.

"Maggie and Joel, together forever," Isla was teasing now, blissfully unaware of Maggie's sinister circumstances. "Has a nice ring to it, doesn't it?"

This time Maggie didn't respond. Her hands suddenly went ice cold.

"Are you still there?" Isla asked.

With a start, Maggie regained her composure. "Yeah, I'm here. Sorry, I just got distracted by what you said." She laughed uneasily. "Forever is a long time, don't you think?"

Isla chuckled. "Whatever. Anyway, Mags," she said, her tone altering slightly, "I've got to go. The doctor's just arrived. I'll talk to you later, okay?"

"Okay. I'm so glad you're feeling better," Maggie said. The tears were suddenly brimming in her eyes again. Her best friend—the closest thing she'd ever had to a sister—was going to be alright. "And Isla? Love you."

Isla snorted. "Love you too, weirdo."

And then the line went dead.

Maggie looked back into Joel's bedroom. She turned just in time to see Joel's latest attempt at a spell fail in a puff of candle smoke. Joel pounded the hardwood floor with his fist and swore under his breath.

Maggie turned back to face the forest. She shivered, though not from the cold. She knew what she had to do. It was the only thing they hadn't tried yet, and it was about time that one of them suggested it. She looked up at the moon. Suddenly, it appeared bolder to her. Brighter, clearer now in the cobalt night sky.

Maggie wrapped her arms around herself and retreated into the bedroom. Joel looked up at her arrival, his eyes lost and unfocused.

Maggie went to him and knelt before him. She took his face in her hands and kissed his lips. He kissed her back, and in that moment they belonged together. They belonged to each other.

They were silent for a while, watching each other's gaze, each one waiting for the other's response.

"I'm not Kaden's," Maggie whispered at last.

"I. . ." Joel tried to speak.

"I'm not Kaden's, because I'm yours. I always have been." She took a deep breath. She'd never been so sure of anything in her life. "And if anyone's going to recruit me," she continued, "I want it to be you."

TWENTY ONE

Invited

MAGGIE GLANCED UP at the night sky, where the moon was staring down upon the Tomlins family's sprawling mansion.

"Time's running out, isn't it?" she murmured to Joel.

He didn't say anything.

"You're afraid, and I don't know what other options there are. Except. . . except for you to turn me into a witch yourself."

Joel visibly tensed. "I won't turn you," he answered tightly. "I won't do that." He grabbed for his journal and began flipping frantically through the pages again. "There's still time."

"How long?" Maggie pressed.

Joel's gaze flickered to the full moon beyond the French doors. He said nothing.

"It's tonight, isn't it?" Maggie answered for him.

Joel exhaled sharply and let the book fall from his hands. The pages fluttered like a bird's wings as it fell. "I'll hide you," he stammered. "He can't take you if he can't find you— "

The look in Maggie's eyes silenced him.

"I won't do it," Joel said again.

Maggie threw up her arms. "If you don't, he will," she reminded him breathlessly. "It could work, right? If *you* recruit me, then surely he can't?"

Even as she said the words, her heart was pounding in her throat and she stiffened in fear. Did she want this? Could she actually live with becoming a witch—or some version of a witch? Could she become a member of the Tomlins coven?

Maybe, she decided.

Or maybe this was a reckless act of desperation.

All she knew was that she didn't want the alternative.

She looked deeply into Joel's eyes. The same violet eyes she'd seen for the past seven years. "You have to," she said simply.

"No," Joel whispered again, stepping away from her, stumbling. "I can't do that to you."

Maggie swallowed. "Why not?" She lowered her eyes to the floor boards. "Don't you want me?"

"Of course I..." Joel stuttered. "It's not about that," he started again. "It's about this."

He flicked his wrist towards the balcony doors and they swung open. Then he raised his arms and a gale tore through the bedroom at his command.

"See?" he said, standing master to the wind as it shook the chandelier and rippled through their hair. "This is what I know how to do. Wind, weather, energies. Not... not what you're asking me to do."

"But what else am I supposed to do, Joel?"

The wind stopped and Maggie's hair fluttered back down to rest on her shoulders.

Joel said nothing.

They stood in silence again, watching each other, waiting for the next move.

"I don't want to be part of Kaden's coven," Maggie repeated. "I want to be"—she looked around the bedroom—"here."

Joel was listening to her, deep in thought. But he was also listening to something else, too. Something beyond her ears. She could feel it.

At last he spoke. "I'm sorry," was all he said.

For a long moment, Maggie stayed quiet. The only sound was the wind tapping at the balcony doors.

"What are you sorry for?" she asked after a while. "Because you won't do it? Or because you will?"

He stepped closer to her, drawing her into him. "Invite me," he murmured. "Say I can cast a spell on you."

Maggie began to tremble as she locked her arms around him. "You can cast a spell on me," she allowed in a weak voice.

Joel gently pushed her hair to one side and began whispering into her ear.

"*Hear my voice,*

The words I plant,

One more breath,

Then sleep I grant."

Maggie inhaled sharply and her lips parted as the air entered her lungs. Her eyes widened in realisation just as she slumped forward into Joel's arms and everything went dark.

TWENTY TWO

Party's Here

JOEL RACED THROUGH the quiet streets of Blackheath. With every pound of his feet hitting the pavement, his heart thudded inside his chest. Maggie had been right; the final hour was approaching and he couldn't allow Kaden to perform the ritual.

He'd tried to save Maggie, and he'd failed. Now he was out of options.

Except one.

He closed in on the abandoned carnival grounds. The fluorescent lights had been turned off for the season, and the rides and stalls were covered with tarps. There was nothing but darkness now. Just how Joel wanted it.

He hopped the gate and paced across the parched soil.

"Kaden!" he yelled, his voice reverberating across the empty carnival grounds.

A prickle moved across his bare arms, like spiders crawling over his skin.

All of a sudden, time felt as though it were slowing down, just as it had done at the party and at the Erridox meal. A moment later, time began moving in fast forward.

It's him, Joel realised, blinking as time restored its normal flow. *Kaden...* For the first time, Joel made the connection. Kaden had been at the party, and at the Errdiox meal, and now...

A figure appeared from the shadows. He was bathed in moonlight, his dark hair stirring even in the windless night.

Joel swallowed. "Kaden."

He smirked as he approached. "I've been waiting for you."

Joel squared his shoulders and closed the distance between them. "Well, I'm here."

"I want my girl," Kaden hissed without missing a beat.

Joel stiffened. "She's not *your* girl."

Kaden laughed, and the chilling sound rippled through the night. The Haunted House loomed behind him, the train dark and motionless.

"*I* marked her," Kaden jeered. "I want her."

"You can't have her," Joel answered bluntly.

Kaden grimaced. "Your spells and tricks won't work. I *will* take the girl and if you try to stand in my way, then my family shall bring war upon yours—"

"Wait," Joel cut in, holding up his palm. "I'm not stupid. I know you're not about to give up that easy. That's why I'm here to offer you a trade."

Kaden's eyebrow cocked and a breeze began to build. The railings around the Haunted House rattled anxiously in response.

"An eye for an eye," Joel went on. "You can't have her... but you can have me instead."

Kaden baulked at the offer. "What would I want with *you*?" he scoffed.

Joel extended his arms. "You can kill me."

Abruptly the wind fell still. The railings stopped trembling and a deathly hush fell over the carnival.

The muscles in Kaden's jaw tensed as he considered Joel's offer. "No," he finally said. "I want my girl."

"She's not *your* girl," Joel seethed.

"I marked her," Kaden repeated tersely. "*You* are worthless to me."

"Oh, really?" Joel flexed his fingers. "But what about the fact that, if you kill me, my power will transfer to you? That's how you recruits get your powers, right? And, speaking as a Chosen One, I think you might be underestimating my worth."

Kaden's eyes flashed with recognition. "*You're* the Chosen One?"

Joel stepped forward into the path of moonlight. "In the flesh," he bluffed.

"But we thought... perhaps it was your brother..." Kaden stammered.

"Who, Evan?" Joel mocked. "Nah. We just let people think that to protect the coven's strength. Sort of like how people wouldn't expect you to be the Fallows top dog, seeing as you were born human and all. Redirection and all that."

Kaden mulled that over for a while, which Joel took to be a good sign.

Before any more questions could be asked, Joel extended his hand. "So?" he prompted. "What do you say? Do we have a deal?" A clap of lightning ruptured the sky, followed by the hollow rumble of thunder. "My life in exchange for hers."

CHARLIE PULLED THE Mustang up outside the old Tomlins mansion and cut the engine.

Dude, this house is creepazoid, he thought to himself as he stepped timorously out of the car. *It'd be cool for Halloween ragers, though.*

He made a mental note to plan next year's Halloween party with Joel ASAP.

It'll be epic, he decided, pleased with himself.

He plodded up the porch steps and rapped on the front door.

No answer.

Twisting the handle, Charlie opened the door and poked his head into the house.

"Yello?" he called. "J-dog?"

Nothing.

It was dim inside the entrance hall. The only light was cast from a few flickering oil lamps that were affixed to the crumbling walls.

"Joel?" Charlie tried again, forging further into the sprawling house to where he could be sure someone would hear his calls.

Charlie was busy thinking about the following year's Halloween fiesta when he heard footsteps creaking along the floorboards upstairs. He looked up to find Evan standing on the mezzanine level above, leaning over the balcony to greet the guest.

"Hey, Charlie. You looking for Joel?"

Charlie broke into his trademark wide grin. "Oh, hey, dude! Yeah, is he home?"

Evan glanced along the upper corridor, then back at Charlie. "I think he's in his room; I see a light on, anyway. Come on up."

Charlie began towards the staircase. "So, E-dog," he began, bounding up the first few steps. Suddenly his foot slipped through the gap in the third floorboard, forcing him to pause to release his sneaker. "I was . . . uh, thinking . . ." Charlie grunted as he grappled to free his foot. Finally he got it unstuck. "Ah, that was stuck in there real good."

Evan offered a sympathetic nod.

"Anyways," Charlie went on, continuing up the staircase. "What was I saying? Oh yeah, so I'm thinking"—he extended his arms open wide—"major rager. You, me, Joel, all the guys, all the girls, party of the century. What do you say?" He formed a thumbs-up sign then twisted his wrists, wavering between thumbs-up and thumbs-down while he waited for Evan's reaction.

"Sure," said Evan, his expression unreadable. "I mean, I'd have to run it by my dad, but . . ."

"Awesome!" Charlie cheered. "So we're on!" He reached the top step and gave Evan a hearty pat on the back. "It's going to be *epic*."

Evan half smiled. "Sure," he said noncommittally, then cleared his throat. "So, Joel's room is right at the end of the hall. The one with the lights on." He gestured to the far end of the long upper corridor. "Unfortunately, I don't really have time to hang out with you guys. I told my dad that I'd help him with some stuff. . ." Evan trailed off.

Charlie gave another thumbs-up. "No worries, bro. I just had some team stuff I wanted to run by J-dog."

"Well, go ahead. I'm sure he'll be happy to see you."

"Thanks, E-dog," Charlie said before marching, heavy-footed, down the hallway in the opposite direction.

When he reached the door at the end of the hallway that Evan had indicated, Charlie knocked once and then let himself in. "Hey, J-dog—"

Charlie's words were cut short and he frowned.

What the. . . ?

The light he'd seen through the crack under the door was emanating from half a dozen flickering candles that had been placed about the floor. There was no sign of Joel, but on the bed lay Maggie Ellmes, sleeping soundly.

"Wah-hey!" Charlie exclaimed.

He quickly covered his mouth, then frowned again when he realised that his loud reaction hadn't disturbed Maggie from her slumber.

"This chick is a deep sleeper," he muttered to himself.

A gust of wind picked up outside and the glass doors on the far side of Joel's room banged against the bedroom walls so hard that Charlie jumped.

Relax, C-dog, he told himself. *It's just the wind.*

Still, he couldn't help but notice that the chick hadn't so much as stirred at the clamour.

Bizarre-o, thought Charlie.

"Maggie?" he called.

Nothing.

"Um, Maggie *Ellmes*?" he clarified in a clear, raised voice. "I'm looking for Joel. Have you seen him?"

Still nothing.

Damn, girl, he mused in approval. *You sure can sleep.*

Abandoning his attempts to wake Maggie, Charlie left Joel's room and returned to the corridor. Evan was no longer there.

"E-dog!" Charlie called.

Evan appeared from behind one of the hallway's many doors. His brow creased when he saw Charlie standing in the corridor alone.

"Was Joel not there?" Evan asked.

"Nah," Charlie replied, then chuckled. "But guess what? Maggie Ellmes is asleep on his bed!" He lifted his palm in a high-five gesture, despite the fact that several metres' distance separated himself from Evan.

Evan ignored the gesture and gave Charlie an incredulous look. "What?"

Charlie dropped his hand. "For reals, bro," he said. "She's in there, sleeping. I couldn't wake her." Then his saucer-shaped eyes widened. “I hope she’s not, like, deadzo. *El deceasediado* and all that.”

Evan inhaled sharply and began pacing quickly towards Joel’s room. When he reached the end of the hallway, he flung open the door.

“Oh, god,” he choked at the sight of Maggie lying unconscious on the bed. “Joel,” he murmured, “what have you done?”

“What’s he done?” Charlie asked, hovering behind Evan in the doorway.

Evan didn’t answer.

The two boys approached the bed and stared down at Maggie.

“Yo, is she dead?” Charlie whispered.

Evan shook his head. “No.”

Then Evan crouched down before Maggie’s sleeping body and hovered his hands over her torso. He murmured a few words that Charlie couldn’t understand.

“Uh, say what, bro?” Charlie said.

But his question was forgotten when, all of a sudden, Maggie inhaled a gasp of air and sat bolt upright on the bed.

Charlie jumped back in shock.

“Where is he?” Evan asked softly from where he remained crouched by the bedside.

Maggie blinked over at him. She seemed to know exactly what he meant.

“Kaden,” she whispered back, her face ashen. “Kaden Fallows.”

TWENTY THREE

It's a Chosen One Thing

JOEL BREATHED STEADILY in and out, watching a bank of mist move slowly across the full moon. He waited impatiently as Kaden paced back and forth in front of the Haunted House.

How much longer is this going to take? Joel wondered, balling his hands into fists so hard that his fingernails cut into his palms. *What better offer is there than killing a freakin' Chosen One?*

He liked the way that sounded. Chosen One.

Maybe I am *jealous of Evan, after all. Go figure,* he thought with a morsel of amusement.

Evan.

Suddenly Joel was hit with a pang of sadness. He was going to die and leave Evan. Not to mention Pippin, and Ainsley too. But what other choice did he have? Kaden had put a mark on Maggie, and nothing Joel did could stop him.

Except this.

He looked back up to the moon. It had almost completely disappeared behind the mist now. Of course he'd thought about Maggie's suggestion—even before she'd suggested it, actually. If only she knew how much he wished she could be in his coven, part of his life, part of him . . . But he couldn't risk her life to turn her into who-knew-what. It was simply not meant to be.

And instead he'd die a hero, which seemed like a pretty cool way to go.

Something buzzed inside his jeans pocket and the Phantom of the Opera theme tune began playing.

Kaden eyeballed him suspiciously.

"It's my ringtone," Joel said, cringing at the sound of the off-key tune. "It's a Chosen One thing. You wouldn't understand."

He withdrew the phone from his pocket and checked the screen.

Evan.

Joel pressed cancel on the call. He couldn't talk to Evan right now. And not only because he was in the middle of bartering with Kaden over his own life, but also because he couldn't risk hearing his brother's voice at the moment. The sound of it might make him rethink his whole plan. Or *think* at all, for that matter.

He couldn't risk thinking right now. Maggie's life depended on it.

Damn my chivalry, Joel mused.

He was about to return the phone to his pocket when the Phantom of the Opera theme began to ring out for a second time.

Again, Kaden frowned.

Again, Joel cringed.

"Persistent," he muttered, cancelling the call.

He quickly typed out a text message to his brother. *Busy*, he wrote.

As he pressed send, he realised that that probably hadn't been the *best* last message he could have sent his brother. It wasn't really all that memorable.

Joel gestured for Kaden to keep on pacing, then hastily began typing out a better last message.

You're the best, he wrote to Evan before pressing send again.

The Phantom of the Opera rang out for a third time.

Stop calling me! I'm busy, Joel typed without thinking.

He sent it, then sighed. That one was an even worse last message than the first.

He quickly opened a new message box and typed another last message. *You're still the best.* He pressed send.

I hate texting, he thought. *Texting is not how I want to be spending my final hour.*

He glanced up to see Kaden still marching to and fro in front of the Haunted House with his fist pressed to his mouth. Joel turned his phone off and slipped it into his pocket.

There, he thought. *No more distractions. No more thinking.*

"Uh, sorry about that," Joel said.

"Your family?" Kaden asked, stopping to observe his rival carefully.

Joel shrugged. "Yeah, but. . ."

"But what?" Kaden pressed.

"But they're not here." Joel's gaze wandered to the Haunted House behind Kaden. To the train that he had watched for so many hours. Its carriages were now empty and its wheels were still. "And they won't come looking for me, either," Joel added. "No repercussions. This is between you and me, right?"

Kaden clenched his teeth and said nothing.

"So?" Joel challenged. "Shall we get this over with or what?"

Finally, Kaden stepped forward and extended his hand to Joel.

"Fine. We have a deal," he confirmed darkly. "In exchange for my marked one, I will take your life instead. Tonight I will kill a Chosen One."

Joel swallowed hard, then took Kaden's hand. This was what he'd wanted, right?

As their palms clasped, the ground juddered beneath their feet, as though the earth was acknowledging the contract. A pact made between two witches, now sealed.

The deal was done. And Chosen One or not, hopefully afterwards Kaden would be none the wiser that he had, in fact, killed just another a regular witch.

KNOWING THAT HE was about to die gave Joel a strange sense of calm, as though he were being released somehow. Released from the pain that he'd held onto for so many years.

Standing there in the carnival grounds waiting for it to happen, Joel realised that he wasn't angry; not at Kaden, or

Maximus, or even his mother. No, he wasn't angry. Not anymore. He wasn't hurt, either.

It's ironic, really, he mused.

What better time to accept life as it was than when staring death in the face? With that notion, he simply let go and gave way to acceptance. To the acceptance of other people, and their flaws, their choices, their demons...

Joel warily looked up to meet Kaden's eyes, wondering what was about to happen. Would it happen in the next minute? Would it hurt?

However, Kaden wasn't looking at Joel anymore. His attention had been drawn to something beyond. Something far off, across the abandoned carnival.

Joel turned and followed Kaden's gaze.

"You have got to be kidding me," Joel muttered under his breath.

Racing past the canvas-covered stalls and between the abandoned rides were three all-too-familiar figures—one large, one medium, and one small.

Charlie, Evan, and Maggie.

Three people whom he really, *really* didn't want to see right now.

"Joel!" they were crying out, a motley and uneven chorus echoing across the empty fair grounds.

Kaden shot Joel a look of daggers.

Joel groaned inwardly and raised his hand in a disgruntled wave. "Yes, I can see you guys," he muttered irritably under his breath. "No need to all shout my name at once."

"J-dog!" Charlie bellowed as the trio neared the Haunted House, panting from their exertion. "And New Guy!" he added, sounding pleasantly surprised to see Kaden.

"What is this?" Kaden hissed to Joel as the others closed in on them. "A set up?"

"No," Joel assured him, holding up his hands in submission. "No, I swear. I didn't know they were coming." He cast a glower at the unwelcome trio. "What are you doing here?" he snapped.

"We're here to help you," Evan answered, his eyes locked onto Kaden.

"I don't need your help," Joel told him tautly. "How did you even find me?"

"Seriously?" Maggie began with a patronising eyebrow tilt. "You're in the most obvious place ever, Joel. This was literally the first place we looked."

Joel narrowed his eyes. "Okay," he said slowly. "So you found me. Good for you. But can you go now, because I'm kind of in the middle of something." He gestured between himself and Kaden.

Evan spoke up again. "We know everything, Joel," he said. "Maggie told us about the mark—"

"That doesn't matter anymore," Joel interrupted him. "Kaden and I have made a deal."

For a second, Evan just stared blankly at his brother. "What kind of deal?"

Joel looked to the ground. "Just a deal, okay? Listen, you guys need to leave. For real."

Nobody moved.

"Go," Joel told them, wincing.

Instead of leaving, however, Evan took a step closer. "Joel, please tell me you didn't do what I think you did."

Charlie looked between the two brothers, his expression clouded with confusion. "What do you think he did, dude?" he asked Evan. Then, turning to Joel, he said, "What did you do, dude?"

But Joel and Evan were only looking at each other.

"I'm sorry," Joel mouthed. "I had to."

Evan shook his head. "No. No, you didn't have to."

Joel swallowed. "Yes, I did," he said quietly, casting a quick glance to Maggie, and then to Kaden.

Evan tensed. "What's the deal?" he demanded again, directing the question to Kaden now. "Tell me *exactly* what deal he's made with you."

Kaden tilted his chin upwards. "In exchange for the girl, I will take *his* life instead," he revealed, aiming his index finger at Joel. The gesture was reminiscent of a shotgun, locked and loaded and waiting to fire.

The revelation was met with a frozen hush while the words hung bitterly in the air, turning to ice.

Charlie was the first to break the silence. "Uh, say *what*, New-dog?"

Maggie pushed Charlie aside and jumped in front of Joel. "No!" she yelled at Kaden. "That's not going to happen!"

Joel gently took her arm and pulled her to his chest. As she fell into him, burying her face in his t-shirt, Joel looked around helplessly at the other faces gathered about. There was Kaden, cold and emotionless. And Evan, looking crestfallen. And Charlie, who was... mostly confused.

"You guys need to get out of here," Joel said again. "Seriously. Please. It's done."

Kaden spoke up now, too. "Go," he ordered the newcomers. "I am owed the Chosen One's life. That is the deal, and so it shall be."

Joel's heart sank. *Oh, crap.*

He glanced over at Evan, hoping against hope that by some miracle his brother had missed that whole 'Chosen One' bombshell.

No such luck.

"Wait, what?" Evan reacted. "Did you say Chosen One? He's not the Chosen One; I am."

"No, he's lying!" Joel cried, freeing himself from Maggie's grasp so that he could face Kaden once more. "Just look at him, man. He's not Chosen One material. He's way too passive."

"I'm not lying," Evan insisted, taking an obstinate step forward.

Now two Tomlins witches were standing before Kaden, mirroring each other in build and in presence, with two identical sets of unflinching violet eyes.

Kaden looked back and forth between them and groaned. "Which of you is the Chosen One?" he demanded. "Tell me now!"

"I am!" the brothers answered in unison.

From the sidelines, Maggie and Charlie swapped a glance, waiting with bated breath—though neither one was quite sure what they were waiting for.

Kaden knotted his hands through his raven-black hair. "Enough! Just answer the question!"

"I'm the Chosen One," Evan proclaimed. "So if you're looking for a life to take, then I guess it's mine you want."

Joel's jaw dropped and he gave Evan a hard shove. "Shut up," he hissed.

Evan looked back at him. "I won't let you do this," he said.

Joel ignored him and turned back to Kaden. "Don't listen to him. I'm the Chosen One, alright? I'm all powerful, blah, blah, blah, so just kill me already."

"No!" Evan shouted. "Kill me!"

"No, kill *me*," Joel countered.

All of a sudden, a new voice came from behind them. It wasn't Charlie's, or Maggie's; it belonged to someone else.

"No," said the voice. "If you're going to kill anyone, then kill *me*."

TWENTY FOUR

Protected

JOEL DID A double-take. "Dad?"

Maximus stepped forward and Joel groaned.

"What is going on?" Joel exclaimed. "So what, does *everyone* know about this now?"

Evan threw up his arms. "Well, obviously I told Dad."

Joel rolled his eyes. "Well, yeah. *Obviously.*"

"Kill me," said Maximus, standing nobly before Kaden and bowing his head.

Joel pinched the bridge of his nose. "Listen," he began, "as great as this new family catchphrase is and all, everyone needs to stop offering to die for everyone else. I'm the only one who's supposed to be doing that."

"Well, if that's the case," Maggie said boldly, "then maybe you should kill m—"

Joel placed his hand over her mouth before she could finish her sentence. "Don't even think about it."

"Bmff wrmm," Maggie argued, her mouth muffled.

Joel turned back to Kaden, whose brows were knotted together in a mixture of rage and perplexity. "You made a deal. And that deal was with *me*."

"That deal," Kaden fired back, "was with the Chosen One." His cool grey eyes looked pointedly at Maximus. "Now I know you know, Mr Tomlins, that once a deal has been sealed, there is no turning back. And so it is written in the skies." His lips crooked into a dark smile. "So, tell me, which one of your boys is the Chosen One? Which one gets to die today?"

"Me!" Joel and Evan shouted in unison, then frowned at each other.

The wind rippled over Maximus, lifting his scraggy strands of white hair and pressing his frumpy grey sweater against his thin chest.

When Maximus finally spoke, his voice was hoarse. "You *can* break the deal, if both sides agree to," he countered. "It's not too late to change your mind. Please," he was begging now. "My boys mean you no harm. I beg you to let them leave."

"Yeah," Charlie chimed in. "I don't really know what's going on here, New Guy, but there's, like, five of us and only one of you. You're outnumbered, pal."

Kaden rubbed his chin thoughtfully. "True," he agreed. "And I could do without spectators. Especially ones of the human variety."

With that, Kaden directed his palm towards Charlie and whispered a single word. "Entrance."

Charlie's eyelids fell shut and he dropped to the ground with a heavy thud.

In dismay, the three Tomlins witches looked on as Kaden swiftly moved onto Maggie. He held his palm towards her and murmured his simple spell.

"No!" Joel shouted.

But instead of sinking to the ground like Charlie had done, Maggie remained standing perfectly upright, a bright gold light encircling her. This time, it was *Kaden* who jolted backwards.

Winded and blinking in shock, Kaden staggered to regain his footing.

"It rebounded," Joel murmured, hardly able to believe it. "His entrancement rebounded."

Evan nodded. "It's because she's protected."

"Leave the girl alone," Maximus called out to Kaden. "She's protected."

"But h-how?" Joel stammered. "I mean, I have been doing a lot of spells lately," he uttered, rubbing at his temples. "But I can't remember doing a protection spell..."

Evan looked at Joel strangely. "Joel. Come on."

"What?" Joel asked, mystified.

Evan's lips parted in disbelief. "Do you really not know?"

Joel shook his head, perplexed, and swapped an uneasy glance with Maggie.

"It's *you*," Evan told him, as though it were plainly obvious. "You're protecting her."

"Huh?"

"Joel," Evan tried again, almost laughing in spite of the tension, "you've been protecting Maggie for years. How did you not know?" He gestured to the air around her. "Haven't you seen the light around her? That's *you*. You're surrounding her. You're... everywhere!"

Joel squinted at Maggie, trying to see what his brother was talking about. He saw the muddy purple hue of fear, and beyond that he could see a faint outline of the iridescent gold shimmer of Kaden's mark. But other than that...

"But if Maggie is protected, then how has he"—he thumbed towards Kaden—"managed to mark her?"

Kaden cackled loudly and the sound tore through the stillness of the night.

"*She* is not the one I seek," he announced with distain.

Joel stopped in his tracks. "What do you mean?"

"What would *I* want with *her*?" Kaden scoffed at the idea.

"You said the girl you marked was from Blackheath," Joel recalled. "No parents in the picture... and then at that party you and Maggie were..."

"My mark was upon Isla!" Kaden corrected angrily. "And *you* blocked me."

It took a few moments for the words to sink in, but when they did, it was all Joel could do not to drop to the ground. Could it be possible that he had made such a huge error? That Maggie wasn't marked at all—and that in fact the gold light surrounding her was some sort of strange unconscious manifestation of his own doing? That the curse was not a *curse* at all? But in fact, a *spell.* A protection spell...

My protection spell. The words played over in his racing mind.

Then a new understanding dawned on him. "The binding spell worked," he muttered. "Kaden marked Isla, and I blocked him."

Maximus dropped his head into his hands. "Joel," he moaned. "You know better than to block a witch's mark."

Oh, hell, Joel thought, clenching his teeth.

"But a new deal has been decided," Kaden went on coolly. "I am promised the life of your coven's Chosen One. And in light of recent... *developments,* I'm willing to bet that the Chosen One is . . ." he trailed off as his finger moved back and forth between Evan and Joel, before finally settling upon Evan. "You," he finished.

"No!" Joel cried urgently.

But it came too late. Evan had already nodded his head in acknowledgment.

"It's me," Evan asserted. "I give you my word, it's me."

Kaden smiled crookedly. "If you're the Chosen One, then you shall die."

At that, Maximus lunged forward.

Kaden held up his palm in a perfectly composed gesture. "Freeze," he said easily.

Maximus froze to the spot as though he really were trapped inside ice. Only his eyes were able to move as they desperately darted between his two boys.

Kaden's gaze travelled from Maggie to Evan to Joel. "And then there were three."

TWENTY FIVE

A Real Plan

MAGGIE WATCHED THE scene play out, unable to move. Okay, so she wasn't frozen in the same way that Joel's dad was—but spell or not, she was paralysed with fear.

She wrung out her hands as she listened to Kaden whispering a string of cryptic words at Evan, and then Joel chanting words at Kaden in response. They had entered some sort of witch-off, and she felt helpless.

What do I do? she thought frantically. She couldn't just stand back and watch this—whatever *this* was—happen.

"Give it up, Joel," Kaden was saying now between mutterings. "The more you try to block me, the more I'm going to make the Chosen One suffer."

Joel kept on chanting.

He's trying to stop him, Maggie realised.

Kaden was trying to put a hex on Evan, and Joel was trying to block it. And Evan was. . . just taking it, she guessed. For Joel's sake.

I have to do something, Maggie decided. *I have to help them.*

But how?

Joel had been willing to give up his own life to save her. He'd protected her without even realising it. And he'd saved her best friend without even realising it, either.

Huh, she mused. *Joel does a lot of cool stuff without realising it.*

She glanced over at him, to where he stood chanting some sort of anti-hex just metres away from her. The Haunted House rose behind him ominously, its railings trembling slightly in the building wind.

Her gaze turned to Kaden and Evan, whose eyes were locked on each other's. Kaden was murmuring something to Evan in hushed tones, too quiet to be deciphered by Maggie's ears. But even from a distance, she could tell it was something bad.

Evan just stood there, proud and calm, presenting himself courageously before Kaden to await whatever fate may be bestowed upon him.

Maggie drew in a deep breath. *Okay,* she decided. *Time to do. . . something.* On impulse, she picked up a rogue stone from the ground and lobbed it at Kaden. It struck his head and he recoiled, his concentration broken for a second. When his grey eyes landed on Maggie, they darkened to black.

Maggie shrank back.

Joel seized the opportunity to communicate with his brother. "Fight, Evan!" he urged. "Why aren't you fighting?"

Evan didn't move.

"Fight back!" Joel yelled, his voice catching.

"No," Evan murmured.

"Please!" Joel begged him. "Please, Evan! I. . ." his voice caught in his throat. "*Please.*"

Evan stood motionless.

Now Kaden's attention returned to Evan. Again, he resumed chanting.

Again, Joel did too.

And again, Maggie returned her gaze to the Haunted House.

Why are they just standing there? she wondered, looking beyond Evan and Kaden and into the grim shadows cast by the Haunted House. *Shouldn't they be helping?*

They had been standing there for a while now, hidden in the shadows. Maggie wasn't sure if anyone else had noticed them yet; no one else had seemed to react to them, so she hadn't reacted to them either. Just in case it was all part of some plan.

Of the two shadow dwellers, she only recognised one.

Ainsley.

The other—an elderly woman with a frail, stooped figure—was a stranger to her. But at least this stranger didn't look afraid, which was a good sign, Maggie supposed.

Through the darkness, the elderly stranger met Maggie's eyes. Slowly, the woman raised her hand, showing five crooked fingers.

Five? thought Maggie.

It dawned on her what the woman was referring to: time.

They need more time, she realised with a rush of adrenaline.

She turned her attention back to the chanting match. By this point, Evan was beginning to look weak, Maggie noticed. He was no longer standing as strong and straight as he had been mere seconds ago.

She cleared her throat. "Kaden!" she shouted, lobbing another rogue stone which sailed over his head this time.

Startled by her interruption, Kaden stopped his incantation and glowered at her. "What do you want?" he snapped, just like she hoped he would.

"Why Isla?" Maggie asked calmly.

For a moment, Kaden's face softened. His expression grew fond, gentle. "Because she is perfect."

In the background, barely audible, Joel's chanting continued. But it, too, was growing weaker, Maggie noticed. She had to keep stalling.

"Then why give up on her so easily?" she called, her stomach knotting as she said the treacherous words.

Kaden smirked. "Believe me," he breathed. "I haven't given up."

Maggie's stomach lurched. "But you made a deal, right?" As she spoke, her voice began to quaver. "Isla in exchange for Evan, right? You can't have both."

"Not yet, no. But once I have the Chosen One's power, who knows what I'll be capable of?"

Maggie could almost hear him salivate as he spoke.

She swallowed, her mouth suddenly dry. "So that's it? You kill Evan, then take Isla too?"

"Ah, so you're smarter than your boyfriend, I see." His smile made the hairs on her arms stand on end.

"But..." she began, unable to find the words. "But that's not fair."

"I'm tired of you," was all he said, flicking his wrist towards her. "Go!"

All of a sudden Maggie felt a surge of bitterly cold air swell around her. But before it could engulf her, the swell rebounded and rushed back at Kaden, sending him stumbling backwards.

"She's protected, remember?" Joel reminded Kaden with the last shreds of satisfaction he could muster.

Before Kaden could regain his footing, there was a heavy clunking sound and he suddenly dropped to the ground, stunned.

Now, in the space where Kaden had stood just moments ago, was Ainsley. The younger boy was gripping a piece of wood proudly.

"Yeah!" Ainsley cheered, bouncing on his toes and peppering the night with a string of colourful profanities.

"Ainsley!" Joel half-scolded, half-rejoiced.

The celebration was short lived, however, as Kaden started to recover his composure.

"Run!" Ainsley cried, grabbing Evan's arm and dragging him towards the Haunted House. Evan followed along behind him, too tired to resist.

Maggie ran to Joel, and with their hands clasped tightly together they set off after the other two Tomlins boys. Clambering over the turnstile, the foursome scrambled along the train tracks into the Haunted House.

In the pitch black, Maggie clung to Joel's hand as though her life depended on it—which, she supposed, wasn't far from the truth. She followed the boys' lead as they raced down the tracks for what seemed like forever before climbing up into an unseen nook in the wall.

Breathless, they huddled silently in their crammed hiding place, listening for the inevitable sounds of Kaden's pursuit.

It was Joel who spoke first. "This was a stupid idea," he hissed under his breath. "Now we're trapped in here."

Ainsley's hand reached out in the dark to punch Joel's arm. "You're a fine one to talk about stupid ideas," he hissed back.

"We shouldn't have run in the first place," Evan pointed out resignedly. "He's owed a life. That was the deal."

"I'm not going to let you die, Evan," Joel snapped.

"Same," Evan whispered.

"Why did you have to interfere?" Joel went on heatedly. "I had everything under control before you came along—"

"Everything under control?" Evan echoed incredulously. "You're kidding, right? You were about to let Kaden *kill* you!"

"Yeah, and you ruined it."

The brothers fell silent again.

Blinded by the darkness, Maggie swatted fake Haunted House cobwebs away from her face. "I'm not sure it even matters anymore," she told them. "Didn't you hear? Kaden admitted he wasn't planning on honouring the deal anyway. He's going to take Isla regardless."

"Not if he doesn't have *actual* Chosen One powers," Joel pointed out, exasperated. "He's only got tonight to figure out how *un*-block himself. Unfortunately, Chosen One over here"—he thumbed towards Evan—"is offering him super-powers on a plate."

Evan exhaled tautly. "I don't care, Joel. I won't let you die. End of story."

Beside her, Maggie felt Joel tense.

"Dumbass," Evan muttered. "You're my little brother. No one gets to hurt you."

"So, what?" Joel spoke again. "You think I don't feel the same way about you, dumbass? No one gets to hurt you, either. You need to stand down. This has nothing to do with you. Tell Kaden that I'm the Chosen One."

"No," said Evan.

Joel groaned. "Just do it, okay, Evan?"

"No."

From across the nook, Ainsley feigned a retch. "You guys," he chided. "Enough with the dying-for-each-other crap already. It's so lame."

Joel and Evan huffed under their breath.

"Listen, losers," Ainsley went on. "You wanna know why I'm not offering to croak for either of you numbskulls?"

"Because you're precious?" Joel offered.

"Nuh-uh, blockhead. It's because I actually have a plan. A *real* plan, not this weak let's-all-just-curl-up-and-die junk that you guys keep putting on the table."

The others held their breath in the darkness, waiting for him to continue.

"She's coming to stop him. And *I* made it happen." Even though his features were concealed by the cavernous blackness, Ainsley's proud smile was evident in his voice.

"Who's *she*?" Evan asked.

"You'll see," answered Ainsley smugly.

Joel snorted. "I know that Topaz tells you she's a red-hot super witch, and I hate to break it to you, buddy, but she's lying."

"I'm not talking about Toppy," Ainsley bit back. "Toppy is just here to summon her. You wait. She's coming. I know she is. We just have to hold out a little while longer and she'll be here."

Maggie squeezed Joel's hand tighter. Whatever Ainsley had planned, she hoped with all her heart that it was something—or some*one*—worth waiting for.

TWENTY SIX

Deal Breaker

INSIDE THE DARK Haunted House, seconds felt like minutes and minutes felt like hours. So, when they finally heard the hammering of Kaden's feet starting to pound down the train tracks, Joel couldn't put a figure on how much time had passed. But he could hazard a guess that it hadn't been long.

The real confusion came when Kaden's footsteps neared the nook in the wall where they were hiding. Instead of just one set of footsteps echoing along the tracks, there were two.

Dad? Joel wondered. *Charlie?* Or was it someone else?

"Kaden?" a woman's voice called out, floating through the channels of the Haunted House as if on an eerie breeze.

Joel's heart skipped a beat at the sound of the voice, and for a second he couldn't breathe.

Say my name, was the first thought that crossed his mind. *Say my name, too.*

And as if by magic, it happened.

"Joel?" the woman called.

Joel felt his eyes begin to sting. He longed to call back to her, but he had no words. Hearing her voice had dragged every part of his being outside of himself. It had left him empty and whole, all at the same time.

Vaguely he felt Maggie's fingers entwined safely with his own. And from his other side, another hand reached out and grabbed his sleeve.

Evan.

"See?" Ainsley whispered. "I told you she'd come."

"Who?" Maggie whispered back.

"Mum," Evan murmured.

Now they heard Kaden's voice, closer than his footsteps had suggested.

"Evangeline," Kaden called out. "What are you doing here?"

She did not answer his question. "You will not harm these boys, Kaden. Do you hear me?"

Joel's heart was pounding wildly in his chest now. He wanted to run to her. He wanted to hold onto her, to see her, to have her be his mother again. It was only in that moment that he realised he wasn't okay without her. He still needed her. He still loved her.

"The Chosen One is mine," Kaden replied. But the conviction that had previously steeled his voice was gone. In its place was something else. Something that sounded almost... purple.

Fear, Joel realised, listening to the vibrations in the darkness.

For the first time that night, Kaden was afraid. But what power could their mother possibly have over him?

Joel listened again to the hum of her energy. She was resolute and angry at the same time.

"You obey me," she said to Kaden, her voice showing no trace of the anger Joel had detected.

"But we made a deal," Kaden snapped in response. "I will be powerful."

Suddenly Joel wasn't sure if the deal Kaden was referring to was the pact made with him—or a different one made with his mother.

"Your deal is broken," she murmured.

"And if not?" Kaden answered darkly.

"Leave now, Kaden. That is my final word."

"No," he spat, his voice quavering.

That was the last word spoken between them. What followed was a blood-curdling scream—though from whose lungs it had escaped, Joel could not possibly say.

IT WAS A long while before Maggie and the Tomlins boys moved. The Haunted House was quiet again, apart from their own raspy breathing.

Once again, they were alone.

Ainsley was the first to speak. "I told you she'd come."

The statement was met by silence.

Finally, Joel asked hoarsely, "How did you know where to find her?" His father had spent years looking for her, and he'd never been able to find her. He'd tried when she'd left after Joel was born, and again after Ainsley, and then again after Pippin was abandoned on the doorstep. One thing Joel knew for sure about his mother, was that she only returned when she wanted to return.

"Toppy told me a while ago," Ainsley said softly. "She said that our mother's been living here, in Blackheath, with the Fallows—"

Joel almost choked at the revelation. Beside him, he heard Evan inhale sharply.

"Have you seen her?" Joel pressed, whispering in the darkness.

"No," Ainsley admitted. "But I can feel her presence . . ." he trailed off. When he spoke again, his voice cracked. "I can always feel her close to me."

Joel wished so much that he could say the same—that he could feel his mother near him, too. But to him, she was just gone.

"Does Dad know?" he managed.

"No," Ainsley replied. "Only the aunts and me. And now you guys."

"Why didn't you tell us sooner?" Joel murmured. "Why didn't you tell *Dad*?"

"Because I know how it feels to know this. And I wish to god I didn't know."

They fell silent again, listening to the stillness inside the Haunted House.

At long last, Maggie broke the hush. "We should get out of here," she said gently.

Joel slackened his grip on her hand, realising for the first time how hard he must have been squeezing it. Maggie tightened her grip in response.

Joel smiled into the darkness and tugged on the sleeve of Evan's jacket. "You okay, Ev?" he asked.

His question was met with silence.

"Evan?" Joel tried again, with more urgency this time.

"Yes," Evan responded at last. "I'm . . . okay."

"And I'm okay, too," Ainsley put in. "Are you okay, girl?"

"Yeah," Maggie said delicately. "I'm okay."

Joel cleared his throat. "And I'm okay. So we're all . . . okay."

In what seemed like one choreographed movement, the foursome rose to their feet and climbed stiffly down from their hiding place and onto the train tracks. As if fused together, they made their way as one back to the Haunted House's entrance. Joel's pulse was racing the whole way, scared of what he might see along the tracks—and terrified of what he might not see.

Where was Kaden? And, more importantly, where was his mother?

After what felt like an eternity, they stepped out of the Haunted House and into the quiet carnival grounds. Joel could see Maggie and his brothers now. He could see their dazed expressions striped with shadows. He noticed that Evan's eyes were glassy with tears, and his heart gave a tug. He wanted to comfort him—to hug him or something.

But for some reason he couldn't.

So instead, he simply said, "Hi, Evan." His voice choked on the three short syllables.

"Hi, Joel," Evan whispered.

Across the carnival, Maximus and Charlie came racing towards them.

But where's Kaden? Joel wondered again. If his entrancements were broken, did that mean that he was...

"You're alive!" Maximus shouted, grabbing all three of his boys in an embrace. "What happened in there?"

Joel leaned against his father's shoulder, unsure of what to say. It was a question he didn't know the answer to. He didn't know *what* had happened, or if it was even over. There was only one thing he was sure of.

"I'm glad you're here, Dad."

And that was something he never thought he'd say.

TWENTY SEVEN

Now You See Me

AS THE DAYS passed and the threat of what had transpired between Kaden and the Tomlinses grew distant, Joel's relationship with Maximus changed immeasurably.

The brothers finally made the decision to tell Maximus about their mother's connection with the Fallows clan, and in the days that followed, Joel felt himself drawn closer to Maximus. Perhaps he'd felt sorry for his heartbroken father. Or perhaps, on some level, Joel knew something was coming. Something that, deep down, he didn't want to happen. Nevertheless, that something was—just like fate—inevitable.

As it were, it happened in the middle of the night. Joel awoke suddenly from his sleep, his eyes popping open with a start. He jumped out of bed and paced quickly downstairs, just in time to see Maximus hovering in the open doorway, looking down the front porch steps. A swell of cold winter air funnelled into the entrance hall, reaching Joel in an icy burst.

Maximus flinched at the sight of his son. His aged body went rigid as his hand tightened around his rucksack's shoulder strap.

Joel swallowed. "Are you leaving?"

Maximus cast his eyes down to the floor. "I have to."

Joel stayed where he was, poised on the staircase, unable to take another step.

"No," he told his father emphatically. "You don't have to."

Maximus looked up at that, meeting his son's beseeching gaze. "I have to find her," he choked out. "She *wants* me to find her. I know it."

Joel had no response. "What about us?" he asked at last.

Now it was Maximus's gaze that turned beseeching. "It won't be forever," he assured Joel. "She's close, I know it. She came back here, right under our noses! And she came to save you. She loves us, I *know* it. . ."

Joel bowed his head. And when he looked up again, Maximus was gone.

JOEL COULDN'T SLEEP for the rest of the night. He didn't even try.

How could he do this to us again? Joel thought furiously.

He sat numbly at the kitchen table, staring out the window into the dark forest beyond. He dreaded sunrise. When dawn broke, there would be no return. Maximus would officially be gone. And Joel would have to break the news to his brothers.

He dropped his head into his hands, breathing steadily onto the table top.

"He loves you, you know," came a voice from behind him.

Joel looked up and glanced over his shoulder into the shadows to find Quite Old Aunt Ruby standing there, watching him with her tiny amber eyes. Her long grey hair caught a sliver of moonlight that was creeping in through the window.

"Love?" Joel echoed. "That man doesn't know the meaning of the word."

Quite Old Aunt Ruby stepped into the kitchen and took a seat beside Joel at the table. She placed her aged hand on top of his.

"Maximus does love you boys," she said in her quiet, mousy voice. "But he loves your mother, too. He always has... and he can't stop. Neither of them can, and they both suffer because of it."

Joel's eyes narrowed and he withdrew his hand. "Pity the children they dragged into their twisted romance," he muttered. "Because it's *us* who are suffering from it. *We're* the goddamn roadkill in their car-crash love story."

Quite Old Aunt Ruby's gaze wandered to the window where the night breeze tapped at the glass. "What do you know of your mother?" she asked distantly.

Joel tensed. "Only that she was human, fell for my deadbeat dad, and then bailed each time she spawned another freak."

Quite Old Aunt Ruby turned to meet his eyes in the dim light. "Evangeline was not put off by her witch children," she said firmly. "In fact, that is the life she sought."

Joel frowned. "Oh, really? She ditched us pretty quick, remember? As near as I can figure, every time she had one of us, she walked away the very next day." He cringed at the pain that was evident in his voice, angry at himself for letting it show.

"Did you ever wonder why she came back?" Quite Old Aunt Ruby asked, raising a silver eyebrow. "Why she ended up pregnant with Ainsley, and then Pippin, too?"

"Because she and Maximus have this screwed up destructive relationship and they thrive off their own misery," Joel muttered.

Quite Old Aunt Ruby mused over his remark. "No," she said, calmly. "They thrive off their love."

Joel rolled his eyes.

"They *are* in love, Joel," Quite Old Aunt Ruby went on. "They have been from the moment they met. But Evangeline... well, your mother seeks the highest power, and the Tomlins clan is just not it."

"Cue the Fallows coven," Joel put in wryly.

Quite Old Aunt Ruby nodded her head. "The Fallows family have power and numbers that the Tomlins clan can only dream of."

"Right," said Joel, laughing bitterly. "And they use a hell of a lot of dark witchcraft to get it."

Quite Old Aunt Ruby flipped her wrinkled palms skyward. "They do what they must to achieve such dizzying heights."

Joel rubbed his forehead tiredly. "So what exactly are you getting at here, Ruby? That my mother skipped out on us and pledged her allegiance to the Fallows coven instead because she was a power-hungry sycophant? Our power wasn't enough for her, so she went to the dark side?"

Quite Old Aunt Ruby nodded again. "In a word, yes."

"And they just welcomed her with open arms?" Joel scoffed. "A human with no power and a whole load of Tomlins baggage?"

Outside, the wind howled through the trees as though it were responding to his pained comments.

Quite Old Aunt Ruby laced her fingers together on the table top. "Evangeline could offer Jefferson Fallows something he wanted."

Joel swallowed, remembering the domineering head of the Fallows clan who had dined with them on Erridox.

What could Jefferson possibly want from my mother? he thought.

And then the answer came to him.

"A human child?" he said grimly.

Quite Old Aunt Ruby's silence was answer enough.

"But..." Joel thought back to the Erridox dinner. "He recruited a bunch of human sons through the Erridox ritual, didn't he? They all seemed so... out of it, except for Kaden."

"Yes," replied Quite Old Aunt Ruby. "All six Fallows sons were Erridox recruits. And yet Kaden, the oldest, was the only one who wasn't hostile to the process—and hence he embraced witchcraft so readily. Which leads me to believe Kaden was raised with knowledge. Raised by a human who knew witchcraft inside and out—a human who had studied it, who was infatuated by it, who was..."

"My mother," Joel murmured.

Ruby nodded. "Not long after you were born, Evangeline surmised that her only way of infiltrating a higher power was to provide a human. So, she found a human man and had a human baby and—"

"Abandoned us for the first time?" Joel guessed. The realisation stung.

Ruby lowered her eyes. "She raised the child, conditioned him, and offered him to Jefferson Fallows when he was of age."

Joel exhaled in a broken breath. "You're talking about Kaden, right?" he said distantly. Then something inside his mind clicked.

"Kaden is your half-brother," Quite Old Aunt Ruby confirmed.

For a moment, Joel was speechless.

Quite Old Aunt Ruby went on, "The other aunts and I have been tracking her over the years. She tried to come back to you, around the time Ainsley was conceived, but by then she was in too deep with the Fallows. She tried, Joel. But, in her heart, the higher power still called to her."

"Why?" Joel choked out.

Quite Old Aunt Ruby shrugged. "I do not know."

"And Ainsley?" Joel questioned. "Does he know about this?"

"Ainsley is intuitive," was Quite Old Aunt Ruby's response. "He knows what he knows, and he doesn't know what he doesn't know."

"So that's how she had sway over Kaden," Joel pieced together in a daze. "Because Kaden is her son?"

"Her son, yes," Quite Old Aunt Ruby agreed with a touch of distain. "And also her key to infiltrating a higher power."

"Where is she now?" Joel pressed. "What happened that night?"

It was a question that had never been far from his mind since the moment he'd heard that blood-curdling scream echoing through the Haunted House.

"She is out there, somewhere," Quite Old Aunt Ruby offered vaguely. "And Kaden... well, we cannot be sure what happened to him. Whether or not Evangeline would harm her best asset is unclear. But I'm sure Maximus believes she destroyed him out of devotion to the Tomlins family—and that she has since gone into hiding to save herself from Jefferson's wrath."

"Is that what you think, too?" Joel asked her.

"Perhaps. Or perhaps she merely struck a deal with Kaden and they are still in with the Fallows, paying penance for their weakness."

Joel looked to the window, lost in his thoughts. Outside, the new day was beginning to dawn and the forest was coming alight with a soft violet hue.

Quite Old Aunt Ruby rose to her feet. "You deserve clarity, what little comfort that may be."

Joel bowed his head and stared down at his hands. "I guess this explains why Maximus is so hell-bent on making a name for our coven." He paused, vulnerable. "Do you think he'll come back?"

"Oh, I have no doubt."

"And my mother?"

"I have no doubt," Ruby repeated with a gentle smile. "Rest now, my angel," she said fondly. "In daylight, all becomes easier."

A small laugh escaped Joel's lips. "If that's the case, then how come you only come out at night?"

"Ah," she clucked, shooting him a gummy smile. "I am not one to choose the easy path. After all, my dear Joel, aren't life's challenges what make us who we are?"

Joel's expression gave way to a reluctant smile. "And who are we?"

"We are who we are," Quite Old Aunt Ruby concluded. She began to walk away, but paused in the doorway. "You will get through this and come out stronger than ever, my dear Joel. I promise you that."

Joel sighed. "Yeah, well, it's not like I don't know the drill."

"And this time," said Quite Old Aunt Ruby, "you'll have her, too."

"Who?"

"Your golden girl," said Quite Old Aunt Ruby with a wide, toothless grin.

Maggie, Joel realised.

"Life gives and it takes, my boy," Quite Old Aunt Ruby was saying now. "Your only task is to enjoy what is given as much as you mourn what is taken. And remember, Joel," she added. "Your story does not end here."

And on that note, she disappeared into the unlit corridor.

TWENTY EIGHT

Normal

"**WHAT DO YOU** know about the Tomlins family?" Officer Bryant asked, folding his hands on the table as he scrutinised the girl in the seat opposite him.

The light bulb overhead flickered, casting strips of fluorescent light across the police station's cold, grey interrogation room.

On the other side of the table, Maggie Ellmes sat rigid in her chair. "Same as everyone else," she replied without missing a beat.

Bryant leaned back in his seat and smirked. "And what exactly is it that everyone else knows?"

Maggie swallowed. "Everyone in Blackheath knows the Tomlins family."

"Maximus Tomlins," Officer Bryant recounted as though he were reading from a personal ad. "Single dad, raising four boys all on his own . . ." The fractured bursts of light reflected in his eyes as he spoke.

Maggie nodded her head, dark blonde waves creeping like ivy over her school sweater.

"Blackheath High kids, right?" Bryant pressed.

Maggie nodded again.

"Tell me about them," Bryant prompted. Beads of perspiration had formed on his brow now; he needed more than this.

"Evan's the oldest," Maggie began. "He's eighteen and a senior. Then there's Joel, who's seventeen. Then Ainsley, who's thirteen, I think. And Pippin, of course. But he's only four or something."

"And Mrs Tomlins? What does *everyone* know about her?" Bryant was leaning forward now, pressing both palms flat against the table.

"No one knows what happened to Mrs Tomlins," Maggie answered. "Only that she cut and run. She left after Joel was born. I heard she came back for a while, but then left again not long after Ainsley was born."

"And?" Bryant pushed.

"And Mr Tomlins went to look for her."

"And then?"

Maggie shrugged. "And he never found her, I guess, so he just came home."

"What about Mrs Tomlins? Did she ever reappear?" Bryant's eyes bore into Maggie across the table. "She must have if there's a fourth child in the picture."

"She came back for a couple of months a few years ago, then disappeared again."

"And, lo and behold, a baby gets left on the Tomlins' doorstep nine months later," Bryant added.

"Pippin," said Maggie.

"How do you know all this?"

"I told you already. *Everyone* in Blackheath knows all this." Now it was Maggie's turn to lean forward. "And I know *you* know all this too, Officer. So I can't help but wonder why you're asking me."

Another lazy smirk. "Everyone knows the Tomlins are witches, too, don't they?" he suggested coolly. "That's why people are afraid of them, isn't it?"

Maggie held his gaze. "Are *you* afraid of them?"

He smiled darkly. "I think a more interesting question is, are *you?*"

Maggie smiled back, musing silently over the question.

"No," she replied honestly. "Not even slightly." She contemplated the so-called *curse* that she had once feared. She was protected by Joel. And now, she would protect him, and his family, too.

Bryant closed his file and leaned back in his seat. "Well, I suppose if that's everything..." He drew out the statement as though waiting for her to add something of her own accord. To divulge a key piece of evidence about the disappearance of Kaden Fallows.

But she said nothing.

"If that's everything," Bryant repeated, "then you're free to go. Oh, and if you happen to see Maximus Tomlins about town, tell him we're looking for him."

Maggie rose to her feet and didn't look back as she walked out of the bleak interrogation room.

What's the point, anyway? she thought as she left the station.

They could interview everyone in town—and they practically had—but they would never be able to pin anything on the Tomlins family because there was no evidence to pin. There were no clues, no forensics to unpick. Kaden and his entire Fallows family had simply. . . evaporated.

As for Joel . . . Well, after what had happened with his mum, the revelations about Kaden's connection to the family, and with his dad leaving too, Maggie had often wondered how Joel would cope. But he was . . . okay, actually. They'd talked, and reflected, and talked some more. They'd gone to parties with Evan and Charlie, and Isla, Blonde Lauren and Hilary. And even cleaned the house on a few slow Sundays. And now things were as close to normal as they'd ever been.

As close to normal as Maggie would ever want them to be.

This was her life.

And it was good.

EPILOGUE

SOME WAY AWAY from the little town of Blackheath, Evangeline waited for Maximus to appear. She knew, if she waited long enough, he would find her. He always did, no matter what. And she loved him for it.

Unfortunately, the Fallows would be looking for her, too.

For that reason, it was not safe for her to be with her boys right now—any of them. But she knew that wherever they were, they were protected by family. Evan, Joel, Ainsley, Pippin…

And Kaden.

They were safe. She was sure of that. But she could not be sure if they would forgive her—for abandoning them, and for hurting them, and for using her powers on them…

For no one but Maximus knew of the particular set of powers that Evangeline had.

In fact, no one knew she had powers at all.

But she did. She had many.

BOOKS BY GABRIELLA

Evanescent

How I Found You

Secrets in Phoenix

The Witches of the Glass Castle

The Witches of the Glass Castle: Uprising

For more information of Gabriella Lepore visit:
www.gabriellalepore.com

Or follow on
Instagram @GabriellaLepore_Books
Twitter @GabriellaBooks
Facebook: Gabriella Lepore Books
#Blackheath

ACKNOWLEDGMENTS

Huge thanks to everyone in the book community. I'm so grateful for your support; Jaspreet, Isa, Evie, Sasha, Ben, and so many more!

Thanks, as always, to my family and friends: Lepores, Nelsons, Carters, Oystens/Wynne-Jones (you don't), Team Chadwick, Xerri, Nikki, Rachel, the Fabulous Saunders of Whaley Bridge, and Westley!

Thanks to my parents, for so much… and so much more.

Thanks to Elizabeth, editor extraordinaire and incredible friend.

Thanks to James, for highlighting the importance of spreadsheets and rounded plans!

Last but not least, a very big thanks to YOU, for reading this book ☺ I hope you enjoyed it!

Love,

Gabriella xxx

CPSIA information can be obtained
at www.ICGtesting.com
Printed in the USA
LVHW091355170220
647181LV00001BA/265